I0624486

FORCE OF NATURE

**Force of Nature Series
Book 1**

Second Edition

By

Kathi S. Barton

World Castle Publishing, LLC

WCP

World Castle Publishing, LLC
Pensacola, Florida

Cover: Karen Fuller
Photo: Shutterstock
Editor: Maxine Bringenberg

CHAPTER ONE

"I'm sorry, Miss Webber. We did try to reach you several days ago when his illness took a turn for the worst. But as he had no number for you…well, I am sorry."

CJ wasn't sure what to say to the man on the other end of the phone. She'd really had no contact with her father for over seven years and his death—recent death, apparently—didn't really mean a great deal to her. She'd written him off, pretty much the same way he had written her off all those years ago.

"Is there anything I can do for you, Mr. Patrick? I mean, do I have to see to…I don't know, arrangements?" She had no idea what she could do for him in death that she couldn't ever do for him in life, but she still made the offer.

"Oh no, Miss Webber. He'd had his arrangements made for several months before his passing. There is the matter of his final resting place, but when you get here we can settle on—"

"Mr. Patrick, I'm not sure how well you knew my father, but we didn't actually see eye to eye on a great many things. And the decision regarding his final resting place would be better left to someone who knew him better." *Or at least cared about him*, she thought.

"Yes, I was…it was hard not to know about your relationship with him in a town this small." CJ didn't doubt that, but didn't say anything. "Well, we could bury him next to your mother, but as I understand it, they had not…we were led to believe that…oh my."

"Yes, that pretty much sums it up. Don't put him next to my mom. You can put him in the trash for all I give a care." When the man started to sputter, she continued. "Look, put him somewhere at the other end of the cemetery. Or better yet, put him in another cemetery altogether. Is that one…Memorial Gardens…is that still in business?"

CJ hadn't been back home in years and wasn't sure what was there now. She'd heard of cemeteries going out of business, but never really cared why. She only hoped this one was still there so she could be done with this call.

"Yes, Miss Webber, it's still there. I believe that would be in the best interest of all parties concerned. Will you…I mean, are you going to be back here in time for the services, or should I just…well, start them without you?"

She smiled at his question. "Yeah, you do that. I don't know when I'll be back that way. You have an address now for any outstanding bills he had. My attorney will know how to reach me again if you need anything else. All right?"

"Miss Webber, your father had done well in the later years of his life. There won't be any outstanding bills. And as I said before, he had already made arrangements for his death, as well as making sure it was paid for."

CJ laid her head against the wall of the building. She didn't really need to hear that right now, but knew that ranting to this man would do her no good. Instead, she simply thanked him and hung up.

Going to her truck, she went to the bed and lay down. She had an eight-hour layover, and her forced rest time gave her too much time to think. She rolled to her side and grabbed the remote for the little television she had bolted to the shelf above her bed. After flipping through the six stations and finding nothing to keep her mind off the phone call, she decided to actually rest. It didn't take her long to realize that she wasn't going to get any sleep.

She had been born Charlie Jane Webber, but had been called CJ almost from birth. Her mom, Rebecca Jane Whitehall, had been thirty when she was born. After years of trying to have a child, she'd had CJ late in life. CJ's father, Charles Allen Webber, was forty, and hadn't been too thrilled to have a child, much less a girl, at that point in his life.

She'd been just independent enough not to bother him too much. CJ seemed to know from the beginning that he didn't much care for her. But as she thought back now, she knew she had tried to get him to notice her. She'd excelled in school, which had only seemed to piss him off. But when she won a scholarship to Harvard, he'd been happy. She'd be gone, and it wouldn't cost him anything.

When she'd graduated with honors at nineteen, he had not come to the graduation and had forbidden her mom to attend. It wasn't until months later, when she'd come home for a visit, that he told her in a drunken rage that he'd expected more out of her than a law degree, and what the hell was she going to do with it, being only a girl, anyway? But what she found out he had done to her mom had her seeing red.

He had beaten her. Not just recently, though that was bad enough, but all through their marriage. CJ had been kept in the dark until she walked in on her mom, who was coming out of the bath one afternoon without her robe, which hadn't been where she'd left it, leaving her skin exposed.

"What happened? Did you have an accident? Mom, tell me." CJ won the tug of war with her mom and pulled back the towel she'd wrapped around her to hide the worst of it. The bruises covered her back, and were all over her legs and arms. "Mom?"

"It's nothing, Charlie, nothing at all." She was the only one who had ever called her by her given name. "Go on to your room and I'll come down soon. All right?"

It occurred to her later that she should have pushed. Her mother would have told her, she knew, but CJ hadn't pressed…neither had she asked again until a week later. That time she'd found her mom throwing up blood, and the bruises were accompanied by broken bones, three ribs. When her mom had passed out, CJ called an ambulance. That was when she'd found out so much about her parents' marriage.

Her father had been hurting her mother from day one. He blamed her for everything, from his inability to hold down a job to their not being able to have a boy child. The doctor explained that her mom had done a good job of hiding it from everyone, but recently her father had become …meaner, he'd said.

"Becky has been in here several times over the past three months. The violence is getting to be more and more dangerous." CJ looked over at her mom while the doctor explained. "If he keeps this up, he'll kill her."

CJ hadn't left her mother's side the entire two days she was in intensive care. She hadn't tried to contact her father, and didn't want him there anyway. When her mom woke up, CJ tried to talk her into leaving him, but hit a stone wall every time she tried. Ready to wash her hands of both of them, she was sitting there wondering what to do next when the doctor came in to talk to her mom.

The blood work had shown an elevated white cell count and they wanted to run more tests. More tests, he said, would help them determine if there was cause for concern or simply a need for a bit more testing. Three days later, they had learned there was no need for more tests. Her mom had cancer.

It seemed as if she went from bad to worse in no time. Within a few hours, they were moving her to Hospice, and when there, they set her up on a drip…to make her more comfortable, they'd said. It wasn't until the second morning there that they did a few more tests and found that her mom had a very rare type of cancer, and that she had had it for some time.

"If found early, we may have been able to fight it better, but now…well now, Mrs. Webber, it has taken its hold, and the only thing we can do is make you comfortable."

"Comfortable? I don't understand. Why can't you operate, or give her chemo or something? Fight it with something?"

The doctor looked at CJ, then at her mom. A message seemed to pass between them that now, years later, she understood. Then, it had only pissed her off. Her mom had known she was dying. Not only that, but she'd known it for several months and had hoped, she finally admitted to CJ, that her dad would kill her and she would not have to suffer. She didn't like him, she'd said, but she didn't know what else to do when she'd gotten sick.

Her mom had lasted another month. In that month, her father had come to the Hospice center only twice: once when she was first admitted, the second time when her mom had requested him to come. CJ had been asked to leave the room. Her father had stayed for a little over twenty minutes, then left. Her mom died three days later after slipping into a deep coma and never waking up.

The funeral was a week later. She'd been instructed to notify her grandmother, her mom's mother. CJ was shocked to find out that she had a living grandmother, and that she didn't like Charles Webber any better than her granddaughter did.

He'd proven how much he hated his daughter at the graveside. CJ had sat next to her father, with her grandmother on her other side. When the minister had said his final prayer, everyone had gotten up to pay their last respects. Phil Campbell, a friend of hers from college, had approached her to wish her well when her father had turned to her.

"She's dead and I'm not going to pretend any longer." The hand that hit her knocked her back against her mom's casket, bloodying her mouth and blackening her eye. "You stay the hell away from me. We're through, you hear me? You're not my kid any longer. I didn't want you in the first place, and now that your mother is gone, you will no longer darken my door."

CJ didn't move when he stormed off. Hundreds of mourners had witnessed the scene, and she wasn't as much humiliated as she was stunned. Phil had helped her up and her grandmother had helped brush her off. It wasn't until she found herself in a limo that she spoke.

"He really hates me, doesn't he? Why? I didn't ask to be born. I didn't...I have no one."

"Yes. I knew that he resented Becky getting pregnant, but I never...I guess I should have known the selfish bastard would do something like this. I'm sorry, baby," her grandmother said before pulling her into her arms. "But you have me and this nice young man. I'll bring you home with me. We'll be fine."

Her grandmother, Angeline Marston, had lived for another four years, and had made it easier for CJ to, not accept her mom's death, but to learn to have it hurt a lot less. *The old bat*, CJ now thought with a smile, had left her everything. As her mom, her grandmother's daughter, had left everything to her as well, CJ had a nice, tidy nest egg.

When her phone rang about an hour after talking to the funeral home, she didn't bother looking at the ID. There was only one person in the world with her number, and that was her best friend Phil.

"The wicked bastard is dead, huh? Are you going to celebrate or just have a huge party in honor of the occasion?"

She smiled at his greeting. "Nah, I thought I'd go and piss on his grave next time I'm in town." She shifted on the big bed. "What's up?"

"Do I need a reason to call my dearest and oldest friend? Can't I just call and say hi, how's it hanging?"

"You could, I suppose, but as I have nothing hanging, as you put it, and you know that I'm your only friend, that doesn't cut it." She smiled when he snorted. "So I ask again, what's up?"

"I bought you something today with your money. You're going to stop this driving shit now, as you promised some time ago, and become stationary so we can have an occasional dinner together. There's even a house in the deal for you."

She had promised him that she'd give up the life of a trucker once her father was gone. She couldn't remember the why of that now, but at the time, she had thought it was a sound idea. CJ closed her eyes and tried to think of a reason for her not to give up the road.

"Phil, I—"

"No. I won't hear anything other than, 'Thanks, Phil. Give me all the details of this wonderful opportunity.' Say it, CJ…tell me what I want to hear. I miss you."

She looked around the cab that had been her home for over six years. She loved her life as a driver, and wondered again why she'd said she would give it up.

"Thanks, Phil." CJ closed her eyes again. "Let me finish this run and I'll be there in a few days. Can you make arrangements to have Grandma's house opened for me? Do I still own it?"

His laughter was what she needed. "Yes…I didn't sell it. But you should know that your mom's house is yours again also. You own it free and clear now. I'm making arrangements to have it sold, if you want. There's a company wanting to buy it that had approached your father about it several times during his life. Of course, he couldn't sell it, but now that he's gone, they have contacted me. What do you think?"

What did she think? Her mother had brought the house to their marriage, and when she'd died had left in her will that CJ would get the house so long as she let her father live there until his death. CJ shuddered to think what he'd done to the house, and was sure that he'd done nothing to maintain it. She'd told Phil to make sure that the roof stayed fit and some other things, but other than that, she didn't care.

"Let me think about it. Send in a cleaning crew and have the place cleaned out of his things. Box them up and give them away, I don't care. When I get there, I'll have a look at it and we'll decide then."

CJ hung up after making arrangements to have him contact the company she was carrying for. As she owned her own rig she could simply go to her grandmother's and stay there with it. She was an independent driver, so she had no contracts to break or any kind of equipment to return.

CJ closed her eyes. She had another eight hours to drive tomorrow to drop and hook this load, and a delivery on the other end to a local company. Then she would be finished. She'd had a moving home for so long she wondered how hard it would be to get used to living in a house again.

CHAPTER TWO

Austin Force looked at the man across from him. Phil Campbell had been a hard man to track down, and even harder to nail down to an answer. Austin wanted that property and he wanted it yesterday. His growing pack had been after that property for over a decade. His father before him had wanted it, and now he wanted it. Wolves needed a place to run, and Austin, alpha of this little pack, was trying to make it happen.

"What do you mean your client is thinking about it? If it's more money, I can tell you right now that I'm already offering you more than the fair market value for it. If he thinks he can rob me then he's got another think coming."

Phil shifted in his chair and Austin nearly smiled. The guy was nervous. Good...the more nervous he was, the more Austin thought he'd put on his client.

"No. No, it's not more money. It's just, with the death recently, my client wants to have a look around. It's a great deal to think about right now. Plus, CJ is a trucker and hasn't been home in some time."

Austin could just see this guy. Long hair pulled back in a greasy ponytail graying at the temples. A beard that would be dirty from donuts and other bits of food he didn't want to think about. He'd wear loose-fitting clothes so that as his ass expanded, he could still keep his pants up over the ample belly he'd gotten from sitting on his brain all the time.

He knew it was a cruel and probably wrong description of this guy, but frankly, he was pissed. He wanted to get this house bought and his mother moved into it before she drove him nuts. *Or nuttier*, he thought with a laugh. But he really wanted the land.

It was rich and fertile, full of wildlife and trees to cover them when they ran. Austin wanted to run free on his land without worry that someone else, someone with a gun, could come on and kill what was his. Old man Webber had been like that. The man had even put electric fencing around his property, like he had something to hide.

The first time he'd met the guy, Austin had been out running. The man had drawn a gun on him and had he been a better shot, Austin would be dead. As it was, he'd only had a few rocks scrape his skin bloody. He'd never been happier to hear that someone passed than he had when the old bastard died. When Austin had heard of his death, he'd done a small jig. His mom had tisked at him, but frankly, he'd been too happy to care. And now this relative from nowhere had come around.

"When will this CJ person be back? I'd like to get things finalized before winter. And I'd like to get the house cleaned up." Austin shuddered when he thought of the state of the house Webber had lived in. "The man wasn't exactly a clean sort of guy."

"Be that as it may, I cannot give you a date until CJ is back. The load that is being delivered now is the last one, then after that it will take about a week to drive here. The rig is CJ's, but the rules of a driver still apply whether there is a load attached to it or not. You will just need to be patient, Mr. Force. As soon as I hear from CJ, I will let you know."

After the lawyer left, Austin sat in his office. This CJ person had better be willing to sell. That was all he could think of. He wondered how this trucker was related to Webber. Austin picked up the paper again. The man's obit read more like a list of transgressions than something one would think to read about in the paper.

He'd been unemployed, but had won the lotto about three years ago. Spending his money foolishly, he'd lost more in the last few months on ridiculous deals and scams than Austin had made all of last year. Winning over seven million dollars had not made the man any smarter, it seemed. In addition to scams and bad deals, he'd also invested in a bar that had gone belly up in the first month after opening. Austin was pretty sure the place was still for sale. The obit had also said he was a widower and had no children.

Austin had his family, three brothers and a sister that he loved with all his life; and then there was his mother and her sister. Austin just couldn't imagine life without family. He heard his brothers in the hall and thought maybe there were days when he would like for them to live a little further away from home, but he still loved them. Putting down the paper, he walked out into the hall to see what they were arguing about.

"What the hell is this?" Blood soaked the front of Connor's shirt, and Gordon looked like he'd gone three rounds with a heavyweight. Neither of them looked as if they were finished, either. He looked at Connor to get an answer. It was that, but not what he wanted to hear.

"He said that he was going to take out Chantal Betts. I had already told him I was going to ask her."

Austin tried to remember who she was, then he looked at his brothers. "Girl with the big...front? Either or both of you could date her and she'd never know the difference. So what's this all about?"

Gordon looked ready to belt Connor again, but only managed to get knocked on his ass by Austin for his trouble. "Stay there, or so help me you won't get up for a week. Answer the fucking question."

"We have dated her. Both of us...the same night, but she likes me better. I told him that I wanted to take her to the movies, and he said skip the movies and just fuck her." Gordon started to rise again, but stayed put with just a look from Austin.

Austin turned to Connor. "And you? What's your beef with his taking the girl out first? And so help me, if either of you tell Mom we're having this conversation, I will personally make your lives a living hell."

Connor flushed. "I hate going second."

Austin looked at both men. They were men at twenty-six, he knew they were, but there were days when he would have sworn they were only ten. Identical twins, women had been falling all over them since they'd figured out that the two of them liked women. Austin often thought they had known that from birth, but said nothing.

"I'm reasonably sure there are more women out there that would sleep with either of you if asked. Why not just find another girl and do whatever it is you want? So long as she is okay with it. If I ever hear of either of you—"

"Never," both of them said at the same time. Then Connor finished. "We don't have to force anyone. They think we can 'cause of our name, but we don't. We know you'd castrate us if we did."

"Damn right." Austin looked at the hall and the mess they'd made. "Ten minutes to get this cleaned up or I'll tell Mom why her flower pot is smashed up."

With a grin, Connor reached out a hand and pulled his brother up off the floor. They both started to set the hall to right when Gordon called back to Austin.

"When was the last time you were laid, Austin? Gotta be at least a hundred years or so."

Austin felt a moment of anger, but let it go. "For that I'm going to tell every woman I know you have a pencil dick and that you can't satisfy them no matter what."

Austin went down to the kitchen to find his mother standing next to the stove, stirring something that smelled like garlic. She turned to him when he entered.

"You do know that I heard every word you told them, right?" Then she did something she'd not done since he was a child...she hit him with the wooden spoon. "Shame on you, Austin Jackson Force. Your father would have been a bit more discreet about his advice."

He rubbed his hand and smiled at her. "Yes, he would have, but then we both know he would have grounded them from seeing the girl too. Fat lot of good it would have done, but he would have done it."

She pulled a large pot from under the counter and began filling it with water. He knew she was building up to something so he got a beer, sat at the table, and waited. But he couldn't get the comment out of his head about his dating...or lack of it.

It had been a while. He tried to think just how long, and decided that if he had to work at it that hard then it had been longer than he thought. Ten, maybe eleven years? At least since his dad had died. He really didn't have time, not now. He looked over at his mom when she sat down.

"You need to get out more. You can't just be here for the rest of your life and not have someone to love."

"I have you to love. I don't need anyone else. Besides, finding a woman who can cook as good as you would be impossible." He took her hand in his. "I'm happy, Mom. Very happy."

She snorted and stood up. "I'm going to start finding you women like this Chantal girl if you don't start finding someone to see on your own. You might be a bit more relaxed if you did get laid once in a while."

Austin really wished he'd timed his drink a little better. The beer he had in his mouth spurted out and went up his nose, flaring up when it hit his sinuses. Between the burning in his nose and his embarrassment, he wasn't sure he'd ever recover. Coughing and choking, he tried to say something to his mom about her and her comment. She simply smacked his hand with the spoon again.

"Oh, don't look at me like that, young man. How on earth do you think you got here? Under a rock?" She turned her back to him and put the pot of water on the stove. "Go and get cleaned up. Dinner will be in seventeen minutes."

Austin got up and kissed her cheek. "Yes, ma'am. And just so you know, I'm not looking for a one night stand, but the one. She's out there. I'm just waiting for her."

"You can't find her if you don't look. You have to look to find the right girl, Austin. Please don't close yourself off. I need you to be happy."

Austin didn't say anything, but hugged her and left the kitchen. He wanted to say he would try, but he knew that it would be a lie. Austin wasn't ready to settle down. Hell, he wasn't ready for anything right now. There was enough on his plate trying to keep his family together.

~~~

Phil hung up the phone. The sale was final, and now all he had to do was convince CJ that this was what she wanted. He leaned back in his chair and thought about her.

CJ was his best friend, no doubt about it. They'd met in college all those years ago and had hit it off wonderfully. They'd dated once or twice, but they decided that it was just not right. When her mom had gotten sick and she'd called him one night, he had listened to her pour out the entire story about her father, and then flew to her side when Rebecca had passed away. The fight at the cemetery had inspired him do everything in his power to make her happy.

He looked at his notes again without moving. She was going to be pissed about this purchase. But she'd told him from the first day she'd become a driver that he had carte blanch on her money.

"Just make me comfortable. I don't want to be doing this forever, so make me comfortable." And he had. More than comfortable…he'd made her very wealthy.

He understood why she'd become a driver. She'd been one hell of a lawyer, but she'd had to stay put to make it work. Her father would always find her, and when he did, he would make her life difficult until she had to move on. Charles Webber didn't want his daughter to be good at anything, so she'd cut herself off from everyone but her grandmother and Phil and taken to the road. Then, when her grandmother had passed away, Phil was her only contact.

Buying the bar her father had failed at was his crowning glory. She would run it, and do it with success. Then when she did, Phil was going to go to the cemetery and piss on the old bastard's grave.

His phone ringing brought him out of his daydream of doing just that.

"Mr. Campbell, Miss Webber is on line one. She said to tell you if you have someone in the office to get rid of her. I told her you were alone." Phil smiled at his secretary. "She believes that you're having a 'nooner,' sir."

Laughing, Phil picked up the phone. "I'm not having a 'nooner,' as you so eloquently put it. I don't have time, what with taking care of your crap all the time."

CJ snorted before speaking. "You should. Get laid, I mean. Might make you smile more. I'm coming back now. I'm about…I think about seven and a half hours out."

"You think you're seven and a half hours out, or you are seven and a half hours out? Either way, I'm ready for you. But since you'll have your rig, you'll have to stay at your house and not Grandmother Marston's. You won't even know the old prick ever lived there."

She was quiet on the other end and he waited. Trying to get her to do something he thought was best was difficult at best, but trying to prod her along only made her more stubborn.

"I haven't decided what to do with it yet. Maybe it's just as well if I stayed there for a bit anyway. Did you get my envelope?"

He picked up the overnight envelope on his desk and dumped the contents on top of it again. "Yes, I got it this morning. How about if we hold off on most of this stuff until you get here? There are some things you don't know yet, and I would like to talk to you about them face to face."

Phil picked up the list of things she wanted done. Selling off the houses was first on the list; the rest of her grandmother's things—stocks, bonds, and her jewelry— were secondary. CJ didn't know that her father had money in the bank when he died, and as his only surviving family, she got that as well. He wanted to talk to her about that and the house she'd grown up in.

"All right. I'll go there. I should be there about two or so if I don't get caught with too many hours. I'll call you when I get up."

"Okay, we'll have dinner together and make plans to meet in the office." He hesitated for a few seconds. "It'll be all right, CJ, you'll see. We can maybe go into practice together finally."

She was laughing when they hung up. He wanted her as his partner more than anything. She was brilliant, and her knowledge of the law still amazed him.

CHAPTER THREE

Austin was on a run. He loved the very early mornings with everything so quiet. He was just rounding the end of his property when he saw the Webber house. It was dark as usual, but there was a big fucking truck parked in the drive. He moved closer to see if someone was moving in, and realized it was this CJ person's truck. Pissed for no other reason than he was, he went up on the porch and looked around.

He could smell that someone different had been there, but not knowing who, he shifted and went to the forest edge to get the pack he had dropped when he'd seen the truck. Pulling on his pants, shirt, and tennis shoes, he went back to the house and knocked on the door, wincing when he realized that he had pounded rather than knocked.

Austin couldn't hear much on his side of the door, but knew that someone was inside. The longer he stood there waiting, the angrier he got. He tried to calm himself, but couldn't think past the fucking lawyer not telling him CJ was back in town, and that this sleazy bag hadn't contacted him yet. Austin kept pounding on the door until he heard someone yelling.

He stepped back when the door was snatched open. Austin was glad that he'd taken the step just far enough back to where he could still hold on to the doorjamb. Christ almighty, he needed to hang on.

17

The furious woman standing there was gorgeous. Even in her fury, she was a sight to behold. A t-shirt hanging down to her knees did little to hide the ample curves and long legs. When the door had pulled open, Austin saw her breasts leap and bounce from the movement, and his cock jumped in his jeans.

"What the fuck do you want? Because I swear if you're here to sell me encyclopedias, I'm going to shoot you right between the fucking eyes." She lifted her hand to brush hair from her face as she snarled at him, and he watched her shirt stretch across her taut nipples.

"I'm here to...." His mind drew a complete blank. Austin couldn't take his eyes off her.

"You're here to what? Drool? Make an ass of yourself? You're doing a fine job if that was the plan. I'm going back to bed." As the door started to close, he remembered he'd been pissed. He grabbed the door before she could close it in his face.

"No. You'll tell me where to find CJ. I have a few words I'd like to say to this asshole. One of which is about not contacting me as soon as he came into town."

The woman laughed. Austin could feel it as though it was heat scorching his skin. Then she knocked his hand away from the door and started to slam it shut. He stepped in just as the door would have connected with the frame.

She didn't so much as move to her left as she leapt to it. The gun was in her hand before he could think to get out of its way. She pointed it at his chest without a single waver as he was pressed against the now closed door.

"You'll take your ass out of my house this minute or I will use this. You're in my house, which means that I could shoot you and get away with it." Her calm voice had the opposite effect on him from what he was sure she'd meant to give. Then it occurred to him what she'd said.

"What do you mean, 'your house'? This house wasn't put on the market yet. And if that fucking ass of an attorney sold it to you under my nose, he's going to have—"

She pressed the gun to his chin, bringing her body within inches of his. "You hurt Phil and I will tear you apart limb by limb. I'm CJ Webber, you moronic ass, and if you're that company that wants to buy this place from me, then you're going to be shit out of luck."

His body reacted to hers...not just her body, but her scent. Need coiled in his body. His beast, close to the surface because he was mad, snarled at him to take her, mark her. *Mine*, was all he could think. She was his and he needed her. Before he could think about what he was doing, he pulled her body to his and turned her so that she was pressed against the door and he was pressed into her.

Her sharp intake of breath only increased his need. Burying his nose at her neck, he drew her scent deep into his body and lungs and closed his eyes. Moving the gun from his chest, he held her hand above her head and licked her pounding pulse. Rocking his hard cock into her, he nipped at her and licked again. He wanted to bite her, wanted to taste her. The pain was a surprise and he took a step back.

His balls felt as if they'd been kicked, which, judging by the look on her face, was exactly what she had done. He moved another step back and saw her fist coming for his face; he couldn't have stopped it if his life had depended on it. The pain this time exploded in his face. He knew his nose was broken the moment she hit him. When he felt the floor rushing up to get him, all he could think about was that he could have handled that a bit better.

~~~

CJ looked down at the unconscious man. She was furious with him and herself. He'd pissed her off royally and then he'd made her hit him. She started pacing the room, trying to figure out what to do next. She supposed she should call the police, but then she'd have to tell them what he'd done…so not going to happen. CJ went over to his big body and searched for a wallet.

Austin J. Force. *Figures*, she thought. With a name like Force, he was probably used to making women do what he wanted. She pulled out a business card and found his name on it, as well as a phone number. She wondered what it meant by "alpha" under the company name of Force Enterprise. A woman answered the phone.

"Hi. I'm wondering if you know an Austin Force? And if you do, could you please describe him for me?"

"Has something happened to him? He's my son and he was out for…he went out early this morning." The woman sounded frantic, and CJ hated that she'd done that to her.

"Yeah, well, he's a little beat up at the moment and unconscious. He apparently didn't think that when I told him to get out, that's what I meant." CJ looked down at the guy as she continued. "I don't suppose you could send somebody to come and get him before I roll his as…butt out on the porch, could you?"

"Of course. I'll send his brothers. I'm sure between the three of them, they can…are you all right, Miss…?"

CJ flushed. She supposed she should have told the lady her name. "It's CJ Webber. I have the house on Mulberry Street. My father, Charles Webber, used to live here. Do you know where it is?"

"Yes, I know of it. My son has been talking to your lawyer about purchasing it for some time now. I'll send the boys to get him. If you'd be so kind as to tell me how he came to be in his current condition, I'd appreciate it."

CJ heard the cold snap of the woman's voice. She knew that Mrs. Force had known her father. CJ thought about telling her she wasn't like him when she looked down at the man again. If it were her, she wouldn't believe it if someone had told her the same thing.

"We had a misunderstanding. He wanted to lick my neck, and I thought that maybe we should get to know one another first. Not that that's going to happen, but still, a girl must have some say in the matter when a guy nearly has sex with her against the wall, wouldn't you say?"

CJ had meant it as a joke. The woman's sharp inhale at the other end made her think she'd gone too far. She was about to say she was sorry when the woman told her the boys would be by soon and hung up.

She went to the room she'd crashed in and pulled off her shirt. A shower would have been great, but she knew from their address that they would be there before she got out. She was pulling on her socks when the doorbell rang. CJ went to the door and opened it to three men the size of trees.

"Sheesh, your mom must be an Amazon. I was worried about you being able to pick him up, but I guess you can manage it."

"Hi," the first one said with a smile. "You're new around here, aren't you?" She was sure that if she laughed at him, it would hurt his feelings.

"No, I used to live here a long time ago. If you guys would be so kind as to get your brother and—"

The woman who came in behind them was beautiful and small. "You must be CJ Webber. I'm Nancy Force, mother of these four. I'm so glad to meet you." She shook CJ's hand like she'd been pumping iron all day and had forgotten that she was a person. "These are my sons, Gordon and Connor, and this is Dallas. He's Austin's twin."

Gordon and Connor looked scary alike. Both were tall and muscled to the point of wow. CJ could see them having fun at everything they did, and doubted very much that they went dateless on a Friday night, or any night for that matter. But it was Dallas that drew her attention. He looked enough like the man on the floor to be his brother, but little else. She could see that he was serious by nature, and she wondered if she was imagining the hurt in his eyes. She looked down at Austin when she figured out their names.

"Austin and Dallas. I take it you like Texas? Nice state if you like it big and hot." Mrs. Force was looking at her oddly as the three men picked up Austin and carried him out the door. "Well, it's been nice. I hope we—"

"Did he break the skin when he bit you, Miss Webber?" The question had been so soft that CJ wasn't sure she'd heard it right. "If you don't mind, I would like to look to see for myself."

CJ put her hand over the small bite. She had seen where he'd scraped her with his teeth, but he hadn't broken the skin. She was suddenly worried about disease, and looked out at the truck he'd been tossed into.

"Do I have something to worry about here? You know, AIDS or something?" The older woman's laughter had her turn back to her. "I don't think this is the least bit funny, you know."

"No, he has no diseases. He can't get them. May I?" She stepped closer and lifted CJ's hand out of the way. "He didn't break the skin, did he? I'm so disappointed."

CJ moved back and stared at her. "I think you're all nuts, and if you don't mind, I'd like for you to leave. I've had enough for one day."

Mrs. Force nodded and moved toward the door. "It's very nice to finally meet you, CJ. I'm sure we'll be seeing a great deal of each other from now on."

"Not if I can help it. Tell your son to stay away, Mrs. Force. I don't want to have to shoot him for trespassing." CJ stood in the doorway as the woman walked toward the truck.

She turned back to CJ before climbing in. "I'll tell him, but it will do neither of you any good. And I wouldn't shoot him if I were you. It will only make him angry at you, and Austin won't be happy about having to punish you for it." Then, before she turned again, she said, "Or maybe he will. I'm not sure about that one. Good day dear."

CJ stood there for a long time after the truck left her drive. Strange people, the Forces. She started to close her door again when she saw something on the carpet.

"Well, shit." She'd forgotten to give them his wallet. She was just going give it to Phil and have him return it to the jerk. Picking it up and putting it on the table, she went to get her shower. She had a lot to do that day, and she suddenly wanted to get going.

After the shower, she felt reasonably better. The boxes that held some of her things were sitting on the floor of the bedroom that her parents had shared, and she went to get one of them to find something to pull on her feet over her socks. She noticed there were other boxes there as well, and decided to ask Phil about them.

She was in the kitchen when her phone rang. She answered it while she pulled out eggs and things she needed to make breakfast.

"I hear you had a run in with Austin Force." CJ put the eggs on the counter before she dropped them, the mark on her neck suddenly burning. "He's quite a guy, isn't he?"

"How did you...? You know, I forget sometimes how small this town really is. Yeah, he came by thinking to have a conversation with CJ, and he was a little put off that I hadn't called him. Wanna explain that to me? Oh, and he seemed to be under the impression I'm a male."

"Is he still? I doubt there's a man alive who would mistake you for a male for much longer than it would take to look at you. I hear that you took care of getting him out of your house fairly easily." His laughter made her grin.

"Yeah, well, he was very fresh. I don't care for being made a meal of. His mom came with his brothers to get him. She was weird."

"What do you mean 'fresh'?" She laughed at his tone. "I'll kill the bastard. No one lays a hand on my friends."

"Calm down, killer, I'm fine." She broke three eggs in a bowl and began whipping them up. "He wants this house big time. Why? Do you know?"

"He wants to put his mom in it. You said she was weird...in what way? Did she make a pass at you too?"

CJ tried to think of a way to say that Austin had bitten her without having Phil go berserk about it. Deciding not to mention it, she poured the eggs into the pan before she spoke.

"No. But she seemed really odd about her sons. It was like she wanted me to know them or something. I don't know, maybe I'm tired. What are the boxes in the bedroom?"

Her sudden change of subject wouldn't bother Phil, she knew. He was used to her style of conversation, and she didn't bother trying to segue into another topic when talking to him. He'd just follow along until she came back around to the topic again.

"They're things the cleaning crew found and didn't know what to do with. Some of them are pictures, plus a few pieces of jewelry that probably belonged to your mom. They found most of that in her sewing room they said. I haven't seen it yet. Is there a lot?"

She thought of the three good-sized boxes and decided that it really wasn't. She told him that she'd take care of it, then moved on to the house and Austin Force.

"I don't want that ass to have this place. He'll have to deal with whoever buys it. I won't be bullied into anything."

"I did a little research on him. Apparently, he and your dad had a bit of an issue. Your dad put up the fence to keep them off his property. I can't find anything that shows the Forces were ever on the place. Your father claimed that they were pissing on his trees and marking them. The police didn't even do much more than nod at him and go on."

CJ sat at the little table and looked at her plate of food. "He...Mr. Force...did he ever get hurt by him? Did my father ever...you know, hit him?"

CJ thought it was unlikely because of the sheer size of Austin, but asked anyway. She still felt the impact of her father's fist when he'd hit her all those years ago. He had hit her mom; she had little doubt that he'd hit other people as well.

"No, sweetheart, he didn't...not that I'm aware of. But he was abusive verbally. According to a few police reports, he'd find Mr. Force and scream at him in grocery stores and any other place he'd come across the younger man. Austin would simply let him have his say then walk away."

CJ pushed her breakfast away, suddenly not hungry. She knew Phil would understand even if no one else would. "Gift the property to him. I don't want anything for it. Make it so he doesn't have to pay any taxes on it either. Send me the paperwork and I'll sign it. I'll be out of here by Friday."

Three days to put to rest any ghosts she might have was more than enough time, she thought. She was grateful that Phil only said he'd take care of it and had not asked her any questions.

After making arrangements to get her a vehicle, they hung up. She went to the bedroom and looked at the first of the boxes. Phil was right; there were a few pieces of jewelry, but the one that made her break down was the necklace she'd given her mom before she left for college, a locket that had both their pictures in it. Pulling the long chain over her head, she finished with the first box, with most of it in the save pile, before Phil showed up to take her car hunting.

CHAPTER FOUR

Austin woke with a start. He didn't know where he was or, for that matter, how he'd gotten there. The last thing he remembered...he groaned.

"Yes, I'm sure I'd feel the same way if I were you. How's your head?"

Austin looked back at his brother Dallas, who was sitting in the big chair in his room.

"Hurts. I must have...how did I get here?" He sat up and felt his nose. Nothing seemed to be out of place, and he knew because of his species, he would have healed by now.

"Your mate called us and told us to come and fetch you home before she rolled your ass out on the porch. Mom liked her."

Austin wasn't happy about the humor in his brother's voice. "She pissed?" Austin stood up and stretched. His mate. Christ, he'd fucked that one up.

"Who? Mom or CJ? Mom's beside herself with happiness. Already planning a Christmas wedding. She seems to think you'll have her...let me see, she said, 'whelping and happy'...well before then. It's the week of Thanksgiving, so I'd hurry if I were you."

Austin looked at his brother when he chuckled. "And CJ? I would imagine she's kind of upset with me too."

That would be an understatement. He'd pissed her off royally in less than ten seconds before he'd tried to mate with her against the wall. He would be lucky if she didn't use her gun on him the next time she saw him.

"Now there is a woman. Did you know that she's Webber's daughter?" Austin sat down hard on the bed again. "Apparently not. I found out from Elise at the grocery. She said that there had been a big fall out when her mother died and he disowned her. Seems to think the girl is back now only because he's dead."

Now what? His mate was the daughter of the man who had tried to kill him. Austin looked at his brother.

"Fuck, this is going to make Mom mad. How far into her plans is she anyway?" Austin stood again and began pacing. "I'll just have to avoid her…CJ, that is. I'm not going to have anything to do with that bigot's daughter. Hell, for all I know she could have the same nutty genes in her that he had."

"Thought you'd say that." Dallas stood then and clapped his brother on his back. "I'm leaving today. I've got to be in Columbus, Ohio in the morning if I want to be back by Thanksgiving. Try not to hurt Mom too much with your announcement."

Austin went into his bath to take a shower after his brother left. With the water running full blast, he looked at himself in the mirror, wondering what had gotten into him to have nearly taken the woman the way he had. Deciding that he'd just ignore her, he figured he would simply deal with her attorney.

He was standing under the spray when he thought about how she had felt against him. Her body had been perfect for his—breast to chest and groin to groin. She wasn't tall, but Christ, she was beautiful.

Long hair that had been tousled from sleep was the first thing he'd noticed when she opened the door. Dark and curly, he remembered how the silken strands felt as they'd slipped through his fingers. Her skin had been creamy and soft; her neck…damn, her neck had beckoned him to bite. Austin had felt his canines lengthen when he licked her pulse point. He wondered if he would have bitten her and marked her if she hadn't hit him.

Austin reached down and stroked his cock. He could still taste her, the rich taste of female. His female had been delicious. Up and down he fisted his cock until he felt his balls tighten up. He wanted to take her, to find her now and press her over something and take her hard and fast. She'd scream when she came, scream out his name as he leaned over her and bit her. Austin moaned and his cock spurted as he came. Hot streams of cum splashed against the wall as he imagined fucking her. Even as he leaned against the wall for support, Austin knew he was in trouble.

He found his mom in the solarium, pruning her herbs and tying them together in small bunches. He'd built the addition for her right after they'd built the house five years ago. He knew she found comfort in the flowers and plants she grew there, and had already planned to have one put on the little house he'd wanted to buy for her. He was going to have to figure something else out. She spoke before he could.

"Dallas left. He told me that you are going to avoid the Webber girl. Is that true?"

Well, that explains her being in here, he thought.

"Yes. I don't need the complication of what she might be as a mate. Plus, I'm not going to be her...how did you figure out what she was to me, anyway?"

She didn't turn around, but continued to snip plants. "She told me that you licked her neck. I've never known you to have a woman be pissed off at you for being...friendly, so I guessed. I'm right then, aren't I?"

"She's Webber's daughter. I can't be mated to a woman like her. You have to see that, Mom. She is probably just as nutty as he was."

She put some parsley in her basket and turned to him. "Probably. I'm going into town to get the last few things I need for Thursday. Would you like to come with me? I still have to pick up the turkey from the meat market and get some things at Pansy's."

He wanted to tell her to stay away from the Webber girl, but knew that if he did she'd see her anyway. Instead, he simply told her that he had work to do. She had been gone about ten minutes when the house phone rang. He answered it on the second ring.

"Hello Mr. Force. Phil Campbell here. I have spoken to my client, and she has decided to sell you the property. She would like for you to give her until—"

"What do you mean she's decided to sell? I thought that...after this morning, I didn't think she'd...what the hell?"

Campbell laughed at the other end, and for reasons he couldn't explain Austin was embarrassed. "Yes, quite. If you would like to meet me in my office sometime on Monday, I'll have the papers drawn up. Like I said, she will need until this Friday to move the last of her family's things out. There is the matter of her rig. She is currently trying to decide if she is going to sell it or go back on the road, so if you could see your way to—"

"She's not going anywhere." Austin flushed again. "I mean, she and I have to talk about some things. She...I'd like to have a few minutes of her time before we sign off on the papers, if she's agreeable."

The silence on the other end assured Austin that he wasn't going to like what the lawyer had to say. That was confirmed when Campbell sighed.

"I'm sorry Mr. Force, but CJ is leaving today. She won't be back until after the papers are signed. Now, as I was saying, the matter of her rig—"

"Then we'll wait. Where is she anyway? I want to talk to her now." Austin didn't want to see her, he kept telling himself. But damn it, he was going to tell her. She was not leaving before he got a chance to tell her he didn't want to see her.

"Mr. Force, I'm not sure what happened between you and CJ, but she's my friend, and if you think I'm going to let you hurt her like that prick did then you and I will have something to talk about. I've tried to be nice like she told me to, but frankly, I'd just as soon knock your lights out than to do what she told me to do." Austin raised a brow at the lawyer's tone, but before he could comment, Campbell continued. "The house is yours, free and clear. The rig that you won't let me ask you about? I'll have it moved tomorrow. Good day, sir."

The phone didn't so much as slam down as it exploded down. Austin was sure he'd still hear the ringing a week from now. He looked down at the receiver and wondered just what the hell was going on...and more importantly, who was the prick that had hurt her? And she was not going to give him the house free and clear...not without an explanation. Austin grabbed his coat and was out the door before he gave any thought to where she might be.

~~~

She walked around the Jewel and decided Phil was right. Not that she was going to tell him anytime soon, but he was. She loved the place, mostly, she knew, because her father had failed at making it work and she wouldn't; but that was only the icing on the cake.

The bar was beautiful even under the inch of dust. The liquor had been taken out, but she could see the bottles all lined up across the back. The glasses, now in boxes in the basement, would gleam over the bar, and she loved the bar itself.

Walnut and cherry, the thing was at least ten feet long. CJ knew that she'd have to replace most of the bar stools, if not all of them, because they looked worn and torn. She also knew that the kitchen was in good working order, but would need to be updated if she wanted to make a go of the food part of the business. CJ knew that she'd have to have the place updated with computers and phone lines as well. Wandering over to the office door, she opened it.

Large and airy with bars on the window, she knew that her father had probably spent most of his time there rather than out on the floor. She had to laugh at the thought of him only being open for just over three months before he decided—or the bank had decided—that he couldn't make a go of it. The matter of unpaid bills had made the bank foreclose.

She walked around the side of the office to the stairs that were there. Going up, she was surprised again at the beauty of the woodwork in the place, and wondered if she would find the same kind of workmanship in the apartment above. Opening the door at the top of the stairs, she grinned. This she could live in.

The open room she'd stepped into was large, and the skylights overhead made the room look bright even at dusk. Hardwood floors were gleaming with wax, and she could smell the fresh scents of cleaning products. The room boasted a wall of windows that looked out over the woods behind her, and if she stepped closer she could see the parking lot below. Walking to the built in wall unit, she ran her hand along the wood and wasn't surprised to find it was smooth and silky to her touch.

There was another door off to her left, but she decided to look at the kitchen first. The room wasn't large, but it was functional. After living in a semi for eight years, she knew efficiency when she saw it, and every bit of space was being utilized in the tight kitchen. There was a dishwasher and even a large freezer along with the stove and refrigerator. Behind a closed door, she found a pantry and a stacked washer and dryer. The butcher block in the middle of the room looked used and worn, and she loved it immediately.

Going to the small powder room, she could see that the same crafter had worked in there as well. The vanity and the shelf over the commode were made of the same walnut and cherry design as in the bar. Even the mirror over the sink was beautifully done.

The bedroom was huge, much larger than the kitchen and nearly half the size of the bar below. The windows had slated shades over them made of the same dark wood as the headboard over the bed. She could see that the bed had been custom made to accommodate the large room, and wondered for a second how well Austin would fit in it. Shaking her head at the thought, she went to the bathroom and was amazed to see that it had a shower as well as a garden tub. Comfort in this apartment had been someone's priority.

Phil had told her she could move into the apartment right away and the bar could be opened in as little as a month. CJ decided to do just that. She could live up here and work on the lower area as needed. As she went to the bed she sat down.

CJ hadn't lived anywhere that was her own for a long time...not since she was in college, and then she'd shared an apartment with seven other girls. She decided to stay there for the night, and maybe for the rest of her life. Depressed more than she wanted to admit, she got up and went to her new car.

Car, she thought as she locked up the bar, was a gross understatement of what she'd ended up with. The big monster SUV had been hers the moment she'd seen it. Black and sleek, she didn't even look at anything else. But she did have the good sense to know how to haggle. Leaving the lot with the thing had been a major accomplishment to her, and getting it for twenty grand under sticker had made her happy as well. Phil told her he was going to take her with him the next time his car went in for repairs. Maybe she could get the mechanic to stop charging him so much. CJ decided to buy him the little red sports car he kept glancing at and trying hard not to drool over. It was the least she could do after all he'd done for her.

The malls were still open, lucky for her. She had fun playing in all the stores, and she spent way too much money. She bought so much stuff at the kitchen store that it was tricky getting it all in her car. The bed and bathroom place had been very nice in that she was able to get all her needs there before going on to the furniture store. By the next afternoon, she'd have her living room ready to use. She would have to come back with someone who knew about televisions and computers, but she was confident that she'd done well on the laptop and the portable TV for the kitchen.

By the time she'd unloaded all the boxes and bags, it was well after midnight. She was just putting the comforter on the bed when her cell went off.

"I just drove by and saw your lights on. I'm guessing you like the place." Phil sounded very pleased with himself.

"Yes, I do. Come back and see what I bought. You are not going to believe how much I spent tonight. I'll order us a pizza."

"Can't. I have court early in the morning. Tomorrow night it's a date, and I don't want pizza. How much begging would I have to do to get a home cooked meal out of you?" She laughed at his pleading tone.

"Not much. How does…no, I won't tell you. You come over and come hungry. I'll make your favorite dessert, though. How about carrot cake with cream cheese frosting?"

"How about I marry you and you simply cook for me for the rest of my life? However, if you cook like that all the time, then I won't live that long. What time?"

They agreed about a time and she nearly hung up when he stopped her. "I had the rig moved today. That Force guy is aptly named. He wants to talk to you. I sort of told him you were out of town. I don't know what he meant, but he seemed to think that the two of you have unfinished business and was pissed when I told him. Do you think he'll hurt you because you popped him in the nose?"

CJ didn't know for sure. He didn't seem like the violent type, but then neither had her father. She finished putting the tea maker together to brew a pot of tea before she answered.

"No. I don't know why I think that, but I do. He was pissed about not being able to talk to me? What does he want?"

"Don't know, love, but he will probably not sign off on the house until you do. Want me to set something up? It won't be until after the weekend." She heard his car door shut and knew he was home.

"No, not now. If he persists then yeah, but not now. If he doesn't want the house then I'm sure we can find another buyer for it." She looked out the window and down into the parking lot. Her rig was sitting there under the lights. "Phil, don't sell the rig just yet. I might not like this stationary living."

After she'd hung up, she went to the bedroom. She couldn't sleep. Thoughts of Austin and him pressing her against the wall kept her awake. Finally, she got up, went into the kitchen, and brewed herself a cup of tea. The man was going to drive her crazy, she just knew it.

CHAPTER FIVE

Austin worked until he couldn't stand up anymore. His fingers hurt and his back was killing him. He'd gotten the chairs done for the Anderson order and the table just needed another coat of gloss. As he ran his hand over the smooth surface of the seat, he could feel his connection to the wood somehow. Eight chairs and two more with arms was a big gathering. Austin was pleased with the work and had enough wood left over that he made a small cabinet and sink for their little girl. It was a personal thing for him that he loved making things for children, and couldn't wait to do so for some of his own pack members—as soon as he got a few anyway, he thought with a grin.

Austin made furniture and anything else that had to do with wood. He loved to design his own stuff and never tired of thinking up new ways of blending different types of woods together to make it unique. It also relaxed him to pull something out of the wood and make it into something.

Force Enterprise had been his father's business, and he and his brothers had all worked for him and with him for years. Force made furniture to last. When his father had been killed ten years ago by a drunk driver, Austin had decided to move on, and his mom and family had come with him. He'd never looked back on the other pack or the life he'd left behind.

Austin was just closing up when someone tapped him on the shoulder. He turned to find his sister standing there with a huge grin on her face and her arms opened wide. Picking her up, he swung her around until she begged him to put her down.

"So, did you miss me? I know I did you. Mom said that you found your mate and that you've decided you're too good for her." Holly grinned at him as he put his arm around her and walked to the house beside her. "She also said the girl beat the snot out of you for trying to mark her."

"Mom talks too much. I did not say I was too good for her, but she's Webber's daughter. I would think she of all people would understand that bit of news."

Webber had shot Dallas one night. Dallas had been out for a quick run about six months ago and had come home with a bullet in his leg. The she-wolf he was with hadn't fared so well, and had died at the hospital a few hours later. Webber had told everyone she was a werewolf and that was why he'd shot her. The trial had never started because Webber himself had died before it could begin. Dallas still blamed himself for her death.

"Don't know, big brother, just telling you what I heard. Is she pretty? Will I like her?" Holly winked at him before she danced away with a grin. "I'm going to love her, I just know it."

Austin looked over at the top of the house that CJ lived in. He had been by the house three times in the past two days and still hadn't seen her. The rig was gone and he'd found himself driving around trying to find it parked somewhere. He wanted to talk to her and he wasn't happy that her lawyer wasn't doing what he'd wanted. Tomorrow was Thanksgiving, and he wanted her to meet his family. Frustrated with himself, he tried again to tell himself that he didn't want to see her only to make stupid plans like having her over for dinner.

He looked at his cell when a text came through from his brother Dallas. He nearly leapt with joy when he read what he'd sent.

Found her. She's at the bar The Jewel. Remember the job we did for old man Carson? She has the apartment upstairs. Good luck.

Austin rounded the house and went to the garage. He'd explain later, and was already out on the street when he stopped to answer his brother.

Thanks. Coming home, or do I have to come and kick your ass again?

His phone rang when he sent it. "No, I'll be there. I have a few things to work out before I can leave." Dallas had something on his mind and Austin knew it.

"Tell me. You know you want to so spill it." He drove toward the bar with the headset on and waited.

"I did a little background check on your mate. You should know that her father made quite a scene a few years back. He hated CJ. I don't mean in the 'I wanted a son and have you' sense, but the 'I really hate you' sense. He apparently beat her mom because she had the nerve to get 'with child,' as he told the courts, and he'd not wanted a kid. He hit CJ at her mom's funeral and told her he never wanted to see her again."

Austin pulled over to the side of the road. "Why? Why did he hate her? I mean, I can see him hating the woman…well, not really. A child, Dallas…why would a man not want a child?"

"He seemed to think with a kid he'd not inherit anything from the family—her mom's family, not his. He was even more of a bastard than we'd thought."

For his brother to say that, it meant a lot. Dallas had sworn that he'd hate the man until his dying day. Unfortunately, the man died before Dallas had a chance to see him brought to trial.

"Are you going to bring what you have with you tonight? I'd like to read it all. I'm…I'm not saying that I'm going to mate with her, but I do plan to see her. We have to talk."

Austin wasn't happy when his brother snorted, but chose to ignore it. After several more minutes of conversation where neither of them said much, Austin told his brother he'd see him that night. Austin started the car again and pulled out into traffic. He pulled up in the parking lot of the bar five minutes later.

There were two cars in the lot; he didn't know either. One was a small red sports car, the other a monster of an SUV, both with temporary tags. He went around to the stairs he knew were in the back and climbed them. He was just about to knock when the door was opened. Phil Campbell stood there with a huge grin on his face.

"She's in the bathroom. I'm betting she doesn't know you found her yet, huh?" Austin looked at the man, wondering what he meant. "Oh, I know your brother found her. Had I not wanted him to, he wouldn't have. Come in."

Austin walked in the door and looked around. She'd made it hers. There was brilliant color everywhere, including the kitchen where they now stood. He walked over to the living room area and ran his hand along the soft blanket that lay on the back of the couch. Austin turned to look at Phil.

"You helped him how, exactly? And what the hell are you doing here all cozy?" Austin flushed when Phil laughed. "Sorry, that didn't come out right."

"I didn't hide her in tons of paper work and false names. That's how her father never found her. I've been around enough to know how to do that. As for me being cozy? She's not my mate, but my friend. You'd do well to remember that, wolf."

Austin felt the small surge of power from the man before him. "Vampire. You're a vamp. I don't understand. How is that even possible?"

"I'm assuming that you mean 'how am I a day walker' and not that you don't believe I can exist. My mother is a vampire, my father is human. I got just enough of his DNA to allow it. And before you ask, no, CJ doesn't know. I wasn't sure at first how to tell her, and then…." Phil shrugged. "Then it didn't seem necessary. Have you told her what you are and what you are to her?"

"No. I'm not even sure I want her to be my mate yet. I need…her father was Charles Webber and he did—"

"Yes, I know. But you should also know that he did worse to her. He never liked her. He wanted her dead from the very beginning. Her mom, Rebecca, was a wonderful woman, if a little on the whiny side. She should have stood up to him. Instead, she let her health go in the hopes that he'd kill her and she wouldn't suffer any more. Unfortunately, or in this case, fortunately, CJ found out and his true colors were shown." Phil sat down. "She's coming now, and for your own good, I'd avoid the topic of me."

Austin turned to the voice coming down the hall. He never stopped being surprised by her beauty and grace. She was on the phone and only seemed to pause a second before she continued with her conversation. He sat down at the table with the vamp and waited.

~~~

CJ didn't want either man there, but didn't want to kick Phil out on his ear. He had brought her a house-warming gift…she just wasn't sure if she should have him return it or if she was going to keep it. Brice Preston came back on the phone.

"Okay, CJ. I got a run going out…nope, won't work. They want a driver with our rig. Can't make that work. I do have…shit, that won't work either. I tell you, girl, if you'd called me two days ago, I'd a had you all kinds of work."

CJ ignored both men as she pulled a pitcher of tea out of the refrigerator. She wasn't going to be polite and offer either of them one, but Austin stood up, took out two more glasses, and poured him and Phil a glass. She was so frustrated she felt her teeth grind.

"What about after the holiday? Maybe I could take a few long distances for you. I have a sleeper cab and my permits are all caught up for crossing over lines." CJ turned away from Austin's raised brow. "I could even leave tomorrow if you need something."

"Well…let me get back to you on that. I do have some short hops we can let you take out. You know how much the others hate them things. I can see if one of the drivers want to give up a few for ya. Can I call you…say on Friday? I'll have things all firmed up for you then."

"Sure, Brice, that'd be great. I guess stationary life isn't what I'd thought it would be." She took out a pen and wrote a maybe next to Brice's name for runs. "I'll look forward to hearing from you."

When they hung up, she stood with her back to the two men in her kitchen and took a deep breath. When she turned around, she thought she had better control over herself. She was wrong.

"I don't suppose you're making plans to visit an uncle, are you? Because as far as you leaving on a long haul, that's so not going to happen." Austin looked over at Phil when he snickered. "What?"

"I think he's trying to tell you to shut up." She picked up both men's coats and held them out. "I'm very happy you both stopped by, but as you can see, I have everything under control and I no longer need a father figure."

They didn't move. She wanted to stomp her foot and demand that they get out, but she was pretty sure she'd only make herself look foolish. She dropped the coats back on the chair and stalked toward the hall again.

"Then stay. I don't give a shit. I'm tired and I'm going to go to bed. When you leave, lock up." She was nearly to the hall when she felt hands wrap around her waist. "Put me down, you moron. I didn't invite you here, and neither one of you are on my buddy list tonight."

Austin sat her in the kitchen chair and Phil put his hand on hers when she made to move. "Don't," was all he said before Austin sat too. "We need to have a conversation with you, and you'll do much better sitting down." Phil looked over at Austin before he continued. "I think it's time we both come clean with her. She needs to hear it from us so that she'll better understand what we want from her."

Austin nodded. "All right. But I haven't a clue what to say or even how to start this. It's going to be one hell of a shock for her to—"

"Hello, right here," CJ snarled at them. "If you're going to talk around me then I don't need to be here for it. If you don't mind, as I was saying, I'm going to—"

"I'm a vampire. He's a werewolf." She looked at Phil as he made his statement, then over at Austin, who nodded at her. "We need to make you understand what we are, because it's going to become important that you know. Especially now."

"Especially now. Now why? No, don't tell me," she told him when he started to speak. "It's because of the zombies, and they won't touch me because of you two. Or I know, I have to know now because…you're pregnant and having Austin's baby. No, that doesn't work either. Let me think."

CJ felt her mind race. She had heard of people believing they were vampires and werewolves, but she'd never actually met one. The other day she had been reading something about dentists who were implanting teeth in the mouths of their patients to make them appear to have canines or fangs. There were even contacts that made their eyes turn to a golden hue or glow.

"He's not lying, CJ. He's really a vampire, though he's a day walker because he's a half breed…no offense meant," Austin said to Phil. "He didn't tell me how old he is, but I would say…well, nearly three hundred, give or take."

"Very good. I'm nearly three hundred and twenty-six. And none taken. I think I look good for my age, don't you?" Phil looked at her and winked. "How you doing, kid?"

"Peachy." CJ got up to pace. "So, you've been my friend for nearly ten years and I'm just now finding out you have an alter ego? Is that what you call it? I'm not sure."

"Hmm, a little tense yet. You'll work it out." Phil got up and refreshed her tea as he explained. "I don't have an alter ego, love. I'm just me."

"So, do you turn into a bat? And you." She pointed to Austin. "Do you turn into a dog or something once a month?"

"I'm a wolf, not a dog. And yes, I turn once a month with the pull of the moon. But I can shift when I want." His tone made her mad.

"Look, buster, you two just told me a wild tale of mythical creatures and I'm supposed to buy it? Back off." She started pacing more. "You guys really believe this crap and you want me to go along with you. I should be locked up. All of us. I think I need a drink." She started for the stairs when she suddenly turned around and looked at the men. "You both should go home. I'm going to be awhile."

She went to the bar and then around to the business side of it. The liquor had been delivered the day before. She had planned to open the following night, with the televisions on to all the games and drinks served all night. But when she had sat down and tried to tell herself she was going to make it, she felt an overwhelming need to run. And then Phil had shown up, and not ten minutes later, Austin. She grabbed the first bottle she saw and started to read the label. She knew the moment Austin entered the bar.

"I asked you to go away. The going away part is out the door upstairs. Not down here where I am." She turned to see Phil come through the door as well. "Now, I know I said leave. I'm reasonably sure that you both are smart enough to figure that one out."

She set the bottle of Wild Turkey on the bar…seemed appropriate since it was turkey day eve. The glasses were all clean and ready to go, so she grabbed one and filled it to the rim. She didn't think a full glass would do what she had in mind, but was willing to give it her best shot. When the glass disappeared, she glared at the two men.

"Put it back. I don't know how you did that, but put it back. I'm going to get drunk and you two need to get the fuck out of my life."

Phil moved closer as Austin circled around to her side. "No. You're not getting drunk. I'm going to touch you, love, and when I do, you're going to go to sleep. When you wake in the morning, we'll work on this again. All right?" Phil's voice was soft, and she could feel herself being pulled under some sort of spell when suddenly, she snapped out of it.

"Stop that. What are you doing?" She put her hand up when he came close. "Don't touch me."

Phil grinned at Austin. "She threw me off. She's always been too smart for her own good. I used a hard dose of compulsion and she simply threw me off. I'm sorry, love, but this is going to hurt in the morning." He was so quick she had no time to move.

didn't know what his plans were, but suddenly she felt him in her mind. The pain wasn't so bad at first, then there was a bright light. Before she slipped away, she heard Austin cussing at someone. *Good*, she thought, *maybe he'll be mad enough to leave me alone.*

CHAPTER SIX

Austin paced the room, which he'd been doing since he'd brought her up here after Phil put her to sleep. Damn blood sucker was going to pay if he'd hurt her. He looked over at the man and glared again.

"You know you're quite good at that. CJ does it better, but you're pretty close." Phil stretched out his legs before he continued. "She will have a slight headache, no worse than the one she would have had if we'd let her drink that glass of Wild Turkey, and you know it."

"You didn't have to put her under so deep, you ass. We still have a lot to talk about, and her sleeping isn't going to fix this." Austin paced some more. "You know as well as I do that she no more believes us than if we'd told her we were going to the moon and back. Now what?"

"We show her...or you do. I'm reasonably sure you don't want me to bite her to prove I'm a vampire." Austin growled. "I didn't think so. You should just hop into bed with her and when she wakes, mark her and then claim her."

"It's not that easy. She is going to be pissed enough as it is when she figures this out. Me claiming her is only going to make it seem more surreal for her." Austin didn't even try to correct the vamp on the fact that he wasn't sure he was going to claim her. "She won't be happy with either of us when she figures this out. Especially you."

47

"Why do you think I told her like I did? If she's mad at me then you're off the hook. Well, a little anyway. You should just shift when she brings it up again. I'm sure that'll make a believer out of her."

Austin wasn't sure if it was a good idea or not. It did have its merits, but to shift with her alone...he was actually afraid she'd shoot him. He stopped suddenly and looked at the other man. "You told her so she'd be pissed at you and not me? Why would you do that? I mean, you've been her friend for a long time, right?"

"Yes. I'm hoping that because of that, she will forgive me. If she doesn't forgive you, well then you're shit out of luck. She might make a good vampire, though. She would have to change to a full-blooded one, though. If I changed her, she'd be less than me and—"

"You go near her with your fangs and I'll stake you myself. She's mine." The words hit him hard. "Fuck. I don't need this, or her. She's going to be a major pain in my ass for a long, long time, I just know it."

"Austin, you should—"

"No. You don't understand. I don't need a mate, especially one that's related to Webber. The bastard should have just died earlier, then none of this would be a problem. I wish that—"

"Austin, shut up."

He glanced at Phil. Austin closed his eyes when he noticed that Phil was looking at the bed. Fuck, he just knew she was going to be awake. Turning slowly, he saw that not only was she awake, but she was crying.

"Get out." He started toward her when she spoke, but stopped when she raised her gun. "I said to get out. Both of you."

When neither of them moved, she fired the gun between his feet. He jumped back and looked at her. "What the fuck are you trying to do, kill me? Put that thing away before you hurt someone."

The gun went off again, this time only an inch from his foot. "I said to get out. The next one is going to be in your head. And I'm a great shot." When the gun lifted higher, he backed up.

"CJ, you're upset, and you might have heard some things that were said that—"

The next bullet hit him in the thigh. He nearly fell to the floor, but Phil grabbed him. He was dragging him to the door even as he heard her screaming at them both to leave. Austin wanted to take the gun from her and beat her ass, but was sure if he didn't get moving, he'd be one dead wolf.

He was out the door and to his car before he could think. He looked at Phil and wondered if he should thank him or murder him.

"You could have told me she was awake." He was sitting in his car and his keys were being put into his hand.

"I tried. When you get on a roll, you don't know when to shut up. The bullet went through. If you shift, will it heal? It's not silver." Phil held his hand over the wound and looked at him. "Austin, did you hear me?"

"Yes, I'll shift and I'll be fine." He looked up at the apartment. "She fucking shot me. Shot me in the fucking leg."

"You're just lucky she didn't blow your brains out. She was really hurt, you know."

Austin looked up again at Phil's words. "Yes. Damn it, what the hell am I supposed to do now? If I go near her, I'm as good as dead."

"No shit." Austin laughed at the vamp's snarled answer. "You know, you might want to spend less time laughing at me and more time trying figure out a way to get her back. This is not going to get you a mate."

Austin looked up at the window again. She was his, his mate, and he'd just given her every reason in the world not only to not trust him, but to also hate him. Pulling his body into his car, he put the key in the ignition and started it up. He needed to get to someplace he could shift and heal. Looking at the vamp, he wondered if he was in with her better than Austin was right now.

"I'm not moving in on your mate, Austin. She's my friend, and always will be. I love her, yes, but I'm not in love with her. I'm going to watch over her tonight." When Austin looked at him sharply, Phil continued. "From here. She won't do anything stupid to herself, but she may run. It's her way of dealing. I'll keep an eye on her. You get yourself fixed up. You're going to need all the extra strength you can get."

Austin thought the man was right. Pulling out of the lot, he wondered if he could have fucked this up any worse, and thought maybe he'd try to keep from going that far. By the time he made it home, the bleeding had stopped. He was trying to figure out what to tell his family when Dallas came outside.

"You hurt bad, big brother?" Austin shook his head and laughed. "Good. She called to tell us that she'd shot you, and that if you come around again, you'll be one dead dog."

Austin watched his brother walking toward him, and decided he didn't need this. He should just tell her he'd changed his mind and she was free to do whatever. But she'd shot him, and as far as he was concerned, that meant war.

~~~

CJ looked down at Phil as he sat in her parking lot. She'd never been so mad at anyone in her life as she was at him. And Austin. Damn it all to hell and back, they'd almost had her believing them. Then Austin had gone on about not wanting her. Well, she had news for him…she didn't need him either. Going into the kitchen, she decided that she was done hiding out and got her coat.

"Going out, love?" She ignored both his question and the man. "CJ, I really need to clear things up with you. You're my best friend and I don't want to—"

"To what, Phil? Drain me dry? Turn me into a blood sucker? I don't think so. Now if you don't mind, I have things to do. I have…I have to go and get me a Thanksgiving dinner for tomorrow."

She had no idea where she was going to get a turkey this late on the Wednesday night before Thanksgiving, but she was going to try. She opened her car door and slipped inside, thinking she'd just get one of those frozen turkey dinners…they couldn't be all bad, they were everywhere. She was just starting her car when the passenger side door opened.

"Get out. I'm not kidding, Phil. I'm in no mood to fuck with you tonight. I have a headache and I have a gun. Not a good combination, trust me." She'd forgotten to pick up the gun again after shooting Austin, but she didn't tell him that. "I have food to buy and…you eat food. How is that supposed to work with you being a vampire?"

She felt sort of smug for figuring that out on her own. He grinned at her then opened his mouth. She watched in dazed silence as teeth elongated and sharpened. She was just about to reach out and touch them when she jerked her hand back.

"Very funny. I've seen those on television." She turned to the steering wheel and started her car to get some control, then promptly turned it off again. "You really expect me to believe those are real?"

"Give me your arm, CJ. Let me drink from you, and I'll prove to you that they're as real as the wolf is." He put his hand out as if she were simply going to do it. "Give me your arm."

This time, she felt the need to do as he said. Her arm wanted to give in and just let him do it. She tried to focus and after a few seconds, she could feel her need to do what he wanted lessen, then more as she fought it. She looked up at him when he laughed.

"What? Why are you laughing at me?" With shaky hands, she started the car. "This is the stupidest thing I've ever heard. You need help." And so did she, she realized.

"You've heard of compulsion, haven't you? Not the sort that stores use when they put those cheap things at the checkout to make you buy the crap, but compulsion." He shifted in his seat as he continued. "I used it on you, just now and in the house earlier. You tossed me off…not easy for a human to do. I think it has to do with the fact that the wolf is right."

"He's not a wolf. You are not a vampire." She could hear the desperation in her voice and hoped that he couldn't. "There are no such things as werewolves and vampires. Please, just drop it."

He was quiet for so long that she hoped he would do just that. Her head was pounding, and she thought that maybe she would be sick if she didn't take something for it soon. She pulled into the parking lot of the grocery store and without seeing if he followed, she ran inside. She was standing in front of the freezer section when she felt him come up beside her.

"You're going to need something to drink with that. Wait here." He suddenly stood there with a two liter of pop. "And some dessert."

The small cake had come from the front of the store they'd passed through. He handed her this as well. She looked around where they were. No drinks were in that part of the store, nor were there any desserts, unless she counted frozen cakes, and that was not what she had in her arms.

"You want something from the health and beauty department? Or maybe something from the section for Christmas?" When she looked back at him, he was holding a box of bright orange ornaments and a bottle of shampoo.

"You got those just now." When he nodded, she looked around again, hoping that an entire section filled with all the items she was now hugging to her body would appear.

"CJ, are you going to freak out or are you going to listen to me?" His voice was calm, exaggeratedly so. "I'm able to move quickly because of what I am. I can get to—"

She lifted her hand and he shut up. CJ let the items fall to the floor and walked away. It was either that or have a nervous breakdown. Walking toward the front of the store, she concentrated on putting one foot in front of the other and not looking around. She was sure if anyone were to stop her to have a conversation with her, she'd go over the deep end.

She didn't know how she got home...she was just suddenly sitting in the chair at her kitchen table with a cup of tea in front of her. Looking around, she felt like something was going to hop out and...well, she wasn't going there just yet. The water on the stove made her feel marginally better. Knowing that she had made the cup of tea herself was somewhat comforting.

If what had happened in the store was correct—and she wasn't ready to believe anything just yet, but just for the sake of argument—if Phil had gotten those items from somewhere nearby, how did he get there and back without her seeing him? And, if he did go to the other parts of the store to get them, then...then what? Then she was either insane...and that was a strong possibility, or...or Phil was a vampire. And if Phil was a vampire then—

The knock at her door startled ten years off her life, she was sure. She nearly walked away when she saw who it was. She didn't need any more "almost" revelations tonight...especially from Austin.

"Can I come in?" he asked when she opened the door. She wanted to say hell no, but decided to ask him some questions first.

"Tell me why you think I'm your mate and what happens."

CHAPTER SEVEN

Austin was sitting in the kitchen when his mom came down. He wasn't in the best of humors, and had he known she would catch him there, he would have gone to his room. CJ had some nerve putting restrictions on things between them, and then expecting him to live with it.

"You look ready to take on the world. Want to talk about it?" She leaned into the refrigerator as she asked. "I'm always a good listener."

Austin got up and took the turkey from her. "No, I don't. Where do you want this? And don't try any of your tricks to get me to talk either."

She pulled out the larger roaster while he began cutting the string away from the wrapper. They'd been having fresh turkey at his house on Thanksgiving since he could remember. He pulled the bird out of the wrappings and threw out the paper. She started getting out the ingredients to make corn bread for stuffing while he washed up.

"Have you heard from your brother yet? I thought he'd be here by now. I wonder what's keeping him."

He glanced over at his mom when she asked. "He arrived last night. She wants to put restrictions on me. No biting and no…and no other things." He nearly told his mom that CJ said they could have sex, but he was to wear a condom or no go. "She asked me what it meant to have a mate."

55

"Here, get out the larger baking pan for me. I need to pour the batter, and it's easier in that large pan. Please turn on the oven while you're over there. What did you tell her?" She was mixing the herbs when he turned to answer her.

"I told her about mating. Not that she's going to be my mate, but since she asked, I told her. I told her about the marking and other males, and that she would smell like me after we…after sex. She said she wasn't going to have that. How on earth could she not want that?" Austin started to make coffee as he continued. "I don't think she believes me anyway. She thinks the whole thing is barbaric. It's just sex and I thought it could be a little fun, but I don't want her as a mate."

When his mom didn't say anything, he looked over at her. She was looking at him as though she couldn't believe it either. He wanted to hug her for seeing his side. As far as he could see things, CJ was the one putting up the barrier.

"Can you open those eight cans of green beans for me? I need to get them on before too much longer. You guys seem to like them when they simmer all day." She turned away, but he thought he saw her frown. "There's also some ham in the bottom of the icebox. Could you cut some up for spices, please?"

"Then she told me that I could stay the night, but there was no way we were having unprotected sex. I told her that it doesn't matter about any diseases, because I couldn't catch anything from her, and she threw me out."

When the pan dropped to the floor, he turned to look at his mother. She looked…well, she looked mad. He picked up the pan and set it on the counter. He didn't want her upset, so he patted her on the back. "It's okay, Mom. I set her right. She knows now that—"

"You idiot. I've never been so…what the hell were you thinking to say that? Austin Force, I'm ashamed of you. Get out of my kitchen!" When he stepped back from her, she came at him with a spoon. "You treated that poor girl like she was a common...a common trollop, and then you come here and brag to me about it? Why, if you were not my son, I'd...well, I'd take you to the woodshed. Of all the...did you think that maybe she thought *you'd* have the diseases?"

"Why on earth would she think that about me? Wolves can't catch things like that." The spoon hit him in the forehead before he finished the sentence. "What the hell was that for?" He'd seen that look in her eye before. It said, "you'd be better off trying to figure it out for yourself rather than me have to explain how stupid you are." He tried to think, but he couldn't get past the pain between his eyes.

"She thinks you should have been more concerned about her feelings than how all this affects you." Austin turned toward his brother Dallas. "You're a dolt, and it's a small wonder CJ didn't bust you in the head too."

Austin glared at his brother. "And I suppose you could have done better? Just what would you have done differently?"

Dallas poured himself some coffee before sitting down. "I would have gone out and bought the damned condoms and been in her bed right now, rather than standing in the kitchen with my mom and brother. You can bet I'd be wooing her, not insulting her about her lack of morals."

"I most certainly did not say a damned word about her morals. I simply told her that I couldn't catch whatever diseases she was trying to protect me from by insisting I needed condoms."

Dallas grinned as he said, "And wait for it...."

It took Austin several seconds before it finally hit him. "Fuck. I told her she was carrying diseases. That is not what I meant." He started pacing. "She knew it too. She's just trying to throw me off my game by—"

The spoon hit his head this time. He started to glare at his mom and had second thoughts. She could be a bit...mean...when the mood struck her. Instead, he glared at his laughing brother.

"You know," Dallas said as he stood up. "I think I'll go and visit CJ. I'm betting she'll be a bit sweeter to someone who doesn't treat her like she's some hooker on the street corner."

"You go near my mate and I'll tear you apart." The words were out before he could stop them, the meaning of them not lost on Austin. "I don't want her, but it seems I'm stuck with her. She's mine."

He knew in that moment that she was his no matter what he did to prevent it. He may have screwed things up with her, he may even have deserved his mother hitting him in the head, but there was no way his brother was touching his mate...not so long as he had breath in his body.

"Then she is your mate?" Dallas looked at him hard. "Then, brother dear, what the fuck are you doing here?"

He didn't know. Austin wasn't sure if he'd even be allowed in after what he'd done. He looked over at his mother, who was holding the spoon in her hand like she'd use it on him if he even thought of the wrong thing right now.

"She was mad when I left. She was really mad. She told me if I darkened her door again, she'd shoot me." Austin glared harder at his brother when he snorted. "What the hell am I supposed to do, if you know so fucking much?"

"Whatever it is, you can't do if from here. Go to the store if you can find one open, buy the stupid protection—and flowers if they have some—and go and beg. Beg like you've never begged for anything in your entire life." His mom finally put the spoon down as she picked up the phone. "In fact, let me call this friend—oh Elis, you're not going to believe it," she said in the receiver. "Austin has found his mate. Yes, I know, I can practically feel the grandkids on my knee right now...oh yes, I do know. Austie would have been about to bust. But he had a little tiff with—what's that? Oh, I couldn't ask you...yes, that would be better, but still, it's the middle...are you sure? Well, you have probably saved his butt. Yes, Elis, I'll tell him to hurry. Oh yes, that's wonderful. I'll send him right over." She hung up the phone and looked at him.

"Mom, I'm so sorry. But this doesn't change how I feel about her. I don't want her. I never wanted a mate. Not now."

"It matters little the timing, son, it's the doing. Now, go to Elis's flower shop on Tenth. She has it in her head that she can help you smooth things over for you and your mate. You just try and keep your mouth shut about the protection and the diseases, please."

Austin reached over and took the spoon from her, then pulled her close for a hug. He kissed the top of her head and held her. Dallas told him to wait there and he'd be back. Austin hadn't meant to hurt his family, but this business with CJ had screwed all sorts of things up.

His brother came back in the room with a box of condoms and handed them to him. "They were a gift at Christmas last year. I'd forgotten all about them until just now. I don't think you'll find anything open at this hour, so go have fun."

Austin hit his brother with the spoon and handed it back to his mom. With a wink, he was out the door. By the time he got to Elis's, he still didn't have a clue what he was going to say to CJ. So far, all he'd gotten was, "This isn't supposed to happen to me." Probably not a good beginning, but for now, near enough, he thought.

Elis had been a member of his father's pack many years ago. She'd been a sort of honorary wolf in that she was never anything but a friend of his mom's. But she probably knew more about their kind than anyone he knew.

When he opened the door, he nearly burst out laughing at the bouquet she handed him.

Roses and daisies fought for room with the greenery and the baby's breath... perhaps three dozen roses, and at least that many daisies. The roses were a deep red to a dusty pink, yellow, and light orange. There were even blue-black ones. The daisies were all white with their bright yellow centers, their petals a white so brilliant that he was sure they'd been bleached. He took the large spray from her only to be told his money wasn't any good.

"You go and woo the young lady. Women like to be wooed. I know I did and your mother... why, your dad was the most romantic man I knew. He'd buy your momma flowers just because the sun was shining, and then on days it rained because it was raining. You do that for your girl. She'll love you all the more for it."

Austin flushed. "She's mad at me right now. I don't think...she's a human. I had to...she didn't believe me."

Elis snorted. "Course she didn't. What person in their right mind believes there are men who can turn themselves into wolves? Majestic animals, you wolves. You go and show her that after she's had herself a wolf, she won't want anyone else."

Austin found himself back in his car before he knew it. Along with the flowers, he had a large box of candy she "just happened to have in the store," and he'd promised to bring CJ by sometime. Austin was in the lot before he thought about how late it was. But there were lights on, so bracing himself for the worst, he went to the door.

~~~

CJ was drunk. Not a sloppy kind, just maybe just a little tipsy. Her giggling caught her off guard, so she tried to stop it only to go into gales of laughter again. She was just trying to pour some more of the Wild Chicken—not chicken...Turkey—into the glass when the door started to make noises.

It took her several seconds to realize that it wasn't the door but the flowers on the other side. Giggling again, she staggered over to let them in. Besides, she'd never had flowers visit before, and she was going to invite them to have something to drink with her.

"Oh pretty. Can you talk? I love you, roses. Come in and have a seat." She reached out to touch one when they moved, and there was Austin. "Oh look, you brought me a dog too. Hello, pretty doggie. Want me to find you a bone?"

He growled at her and she giggled again. Taking the flowers and setting them on the chair, she sat across from them. But then she realized she'd not gotten them a glass. She started to stand up again only to stagger a bit.

"Oops. I got me feet...my feet all messed up. I just need to get a glass so you can have some too." She looked up at Austin. "So do you want me to get you a bowl of Wild Chicken? I like that name better than Turkey. Gobble gobble."

He leaned in and sniffed her. CJ had no idea why that would make her all melty, but it did. She leaned into him, and he suddenly pushed her away from him.

"You certainly run cold and colder, don'tcha? Let me go, please. I have a guest. The flowers are nicer...is that chocolate? I love chocolate."

"You're drunk," he snapped at her. Then he picked up her bottle. "Did you drink all this?"

"Course I did. I had to have my turkey dinner, didn't I? I dropped mine when Phil did his speedy thingy." She took the box of candy from him and went to the table. "And now I can have my dessert."

She was just pouring another glass of gobble gobble when Austin took her bottle. "Hey! Give me that back. I offered you a bone. Me and the flowers are gonna have a cella...celler...party. And you aren't invited. Go home. Or do you live in a cave?"

She'd been thinking about him and his living arrangements too much, she thought. Actually, not so much where he lived but how he slept. She really wondered if he slept in the raw. After he had left last night, she'd hoped he'd come back with a condom, or a case of them. But he hadn't. That's when she'd gone back down to the bar and gotten another bottle.

When Austin started pouring the rest of the liquor down the sink, she stood up, and that's when she noticed the box on the counter. She picked it up and read the description. The words "extra-large" caught her eye, then the claim "for her enjoyment." She looked up at him when he cleared his throat.

He looked every bit the wolf he claimed he was. His eyes, a warm brown normally, were now a dark, almost black. His face looked tense, like whatever he was holding back was causing him intense pain. Looking down his body, she felt her own react, sort of swell with need of her own. But when she looked at his groin, she moaned and stepped toward him.

He put out a hand and she simply moved it away and put her hand on his cock. She felt it harden beneath her. When he covered hers with his own hand, she leaned into him and did what he had done to her…she licked his neck. When he jerked her away from him, she stared at him.

"You're drunk. And we aren't doing this," he snarled with a shake of her shoulders. "I won't have you claiming later that I took advantage of you."

A slap couldn't have sobered her more quickly. She felt the pain of his words rip through her and was suddenly glad he had stopped her. With as much dignity as she could summon, CJ walked to the door and opened it. She could feel the tears fill her eyes and moved away toward her room.

"Lock the door on your way out, please. Have a nice Thanksgiving," she told him quietly. "And don't forget your protection when you leave."

CHAPTER EIGHT

Austin stood in the dark kitchen. He didn't want to leave, and he knew if he left her, he'd never get to come back...she'd make sure of that. He did the only thing he could think of. He put the box of condoms in his jacket pocket and went to her room.

He wasn't surprised to find the door locked. A simple foot to the lock fixed that issue very nicely. She was standing near the window and turned when he entered. He began unbuttoning his shirt as he spoke.

"You are going to bed now, I take it? I sleep in the nude, but for tonight, just because I'm not going to take advantage of you while you're inebriated, I will leave on my briefs." He pulled off his t-shirt after he'd removed his shirt.

"You so are not sleeping in my bed. You just put your shirt back on and get out." He watched her swallow hard before she continued. "This is not funny, Austin. I mean it, get out."

"No. After we get a good night's sleep, you and I are going to my house to have dinner with my family. I think it's important that you like them, don't you? I mean, we will be spending the rest of our lives together."

"I'm not spending any time with you. You are replacing my door too." She moved toward the bathroom and he pressed her against it when she opened it, slamming it shut again. "Let go of me."

He rocked his cock against her ass and smiled when she shuddered. "You want me, don't you, CJ? And don't lie to me. I can smell your arousal as sweet as perfume."

"So what? I'm horny. You think you're the only one who can want to be fucked? I was just on my way out to take care of that when you—"

He jerked her around to face him. "You'll be careful what you say, CJ. Alphas are an extremely jealous species. And when another male, whether knowing or not, touches what's his, he will kill them."

His mouth covered hers. She was hot, her mouth hard beneath his. Shifting her so that the length of her fit against him, Austin felt her respond by degrees. Her body softened and her arms came up around his shoulders. He wanted her, now. Moving her so that he could lift her, he carried her back to the bed. When he glanced to the kitchen, only to see if the door was locked, he spied the bottle of whiskey on the table. Everything in him chilled.

He set her on the floor and pulled her from him. He wouldn't take her this way…not with the possibility of her not being of sound mind to consent. When she looked up at him, her eyes dark with need, he pushed her further away.

"Austin? What? What is it?" He nearly did take her then. Her voice was so husky he nearly tossed her to the bed and said to hell with morals. But instead, he took another step back.

"No. Not like this…not with half a bottle of whiskey in you. We'll sleep, then tomorrow, we'll discuss this." He turned away from her, away from temptation.

His cock ached, and he knew she could see how much he wanted her. Moving toward the bathroom, he decided that the best thing he could do was jerk off. Give himself some relief. When he returned, he'd be able to sleep the few hours until they got to his home, and then they'd talk. Yeah, he thought, and monkeys would fly.

He shut the door behind him and leaned on the sink. Turning on the cold water, he rubbed his hand down his cock and thought about what it would feel like buried deep inside of her. The thought of coming deep in her made him groan. Closing his eyes, he released his cock from his shorts. He was just wrapping his fingers tight around himself when the door opened.

~~~

CJ nearly turned around and left the tiny bath when she saw what he was doing, but found she couldn't. She watched as he wrapped his hand around his cock and moved it up and down. She couldn't help the moan that spilled over her suddenly dry lips.

"You stand there watching me and I'm going to come all over you." She looked up at his face when he spoke. "Come here, CJ. Help me come."

She moved toward him even as he took her hand and rubbed it against his shaft. She wrapped her fingers around him as he'd done and squeezed him. He jumped in her hand. When his free hand moved behind her neck and brought her close, she moaned again as she felt his mouth nip at her neck.

"Strip. Take your clothes off and let me taste you. Christ, I want to fuck you with my tongue." His hands were everywhere. Her clothes were torn from her even as she felt his mouth on her breasts. "Feed me, CJ. Feed me your nipples while I fuck your hand."

When her breast was free, she lifted it up to his mouth and his teeth sank deep into her nipple, making her cry out. When he turned her around and sat her on the counter, she whimpered when he freed his cock from her hand. But his fingers sliding into her pussy made her forget everything but what he was doing to her.

"I'm going to eat you, suck your pussy until you come in my mouth. Then I'm going to lap every bit of your cum in my mouth, making you come and come again."

"Please, Austin. Please." When he got down onto his knees and pulled her ass forward until her pussy was right on the edge, she watched his head lower to her. "Austin, please, I—"

His tongue entered her. She felt it moved inside, in and out, in and out. When he licked her clit, she threw back her head and lifted up to get him deeper. She wrapped her fingers in his hair and tried to guide him to her clit again, but he wouldn't.

When he finally took her clit into his mouth and sucked her hard, she screamed out her release. His fingers entered her and again, he touched off another climax, then another. She lay back when he stood, his cock thick and hard before her.

"Watch me. Watch what I want to do when I come inside of you." His hand fisted his cock and stroked it once, twice, then a third time before he came. Thick, hot cum jettisoned out from him and onto her belly, breasts, and face. He roared with each release, and when he reached down and pinched her clit, she came again, screaming out his name as he rubbed his cum all over her.

She couldn't move. She wasn't even sure she wanted to. CJ opened one eye to look at Austin. He looked like he couldn't move either. Then he reached into the shower stall and turned on the water. Steam rolled from the curtain as the bathroom heated up. When he stood up from the wall, she didn't know whether to be frightened or not when he came toward her. But he simply picked her up in his arms and pulled her into the shower with him.

The water was almost too hot at first, but her body soon adjusted to it. When he put her down, CJ leaned against the tile wall and watched as he adjusted the spray toward the wall and not directly on them. When she reached for the bottle of soap, he took it from her and squirted it in the large, poofy sponge he'd taken from around the nozzle. He turned her so that her back was to his chest and began washing her.

"You have such beautiful skin. Soft and smooth, like a silk blanket my mother used to lay on the back of the couch." Austin rubbed the poof over her breasts and she moaned as he continued. "And your taste. Nothing has ever tasted so delicious to me. As soon as you sell this place and move in with us, I'm going to make it a point to taste you every day."

It took his words a few seconds to sink in. Sell this place? She wasn't aware that she'd mentioned wanting to sell. She started to ask him where he'd gotten that idea when he moved on to other things he'd assumed she was going to agree to.

"The rig will have to go. I would hate for it to sit and not let someone get any use of it. I know this guy who can get us a good price for it. I'll do that after the weekend. The car I like. Did Phil help you with that?" As if she couldn't make a decision on her own, but before she could tell him she'd purchased that little number herself, he moved on. "We'll have children right away. That'll give you something to do when I'm working. I'd hate for you to get bored. My mother had some things she did when we were smaller, but—"

CJ turned in toward him then, having heard enough. She looked up at his smile and wondered what century this man had come from. She took the shampoo from him when it looked like he was going to wash her hair. He tried to take it back, but she shoved him back hard.

"I'm quite capable of washing myself, thanks. And for the record, I picked out the car. Phil wanted the little red one he drives." She lathered up her hair then rinsed before continuing. "I'm not selling my rig, nor am I having any kids. Not now, maybe not ever. As for—"

"CJ, you can't be serious. Just let me handle things and you'll see that I'm right. I've been...."

She wondered why he stopped and hoped it had to do with the look she was giving him, because she was giving him the best pissed off look she could manage. Shutting off the water, she stepped out of the tub and grabbed the only towel there. Moving out of the room and into the bedroom, she heard him swear and she smiled, despite how pissed she was. By the time he came out of the bathroom, she was pulling a t-shirt over her head and had her socks and jeans in her hand.

"As for the rest of your assumptions, you, my fine sir, can fuck the hell off," she told him as she left him to scramble around picking up his clothes.

The ringing phone had her detour from the living room to the kitchen. She snatched up the phone on the third ring. Without looking at the caller ID, she answered with a snarled, "Hello."

"Oh dear, he's gone and done something incredibly stupid, hasn't he? I'm so sorry, dear. I did try to raise him right." CJ wasn't sure who the person was on the other end, but if she was talking about Austin, she couldn't agree more. "May I speak to Austin, please? It's his mother."

Closing her eyes, CJ felt both embarrassment and mortification. Before she could apologize, the bane of her existence right now walked into the room. Austin looked as mad as she felt, but she was sure hers was more justified. Before he could say a word—which, if his look was any indication, was going to be a doozy—she held the phone out to him.

"It's your mother, or so she claims. Which surprises me on so many levels, because I would have sworn you were shit on a rock in hell and the heat hatched you." He growled at her before taking the receiver. "Be nice or I think she'll hurt you."

CJ left the room as she heard him snarl. She laughed out loud when she heard him change his tone and tune when he listened for a second or two. Grabbing up her coat and keys, she went down through the bar and out of the building toward her car, pulling on the rest of her clothes as she went.

But she went to her rig instead. It took her only a few minutes to remember how much she'd missed the thing, and she started it up. She was pulling out of the lot when he came tearing out the door from the apartment upstairs. As she drove past him and out of the lot, she blew him a kiss and saluted him with her middle finger.

CJ drove around for an hour before she realized she was crying. It wasn't long until she found a trucker's gas stop and pulled in. She was filling up her tank when her phone vibrated in her pocket. She finished pumping then went in to pay before she pulled it out to check. CJ was surprised to see that she'd missed a lot of calls and messages.

Phil had called eleven times and left messages each time. There were also seventeen text messages from him, and a call from an unknown. She read three of the texts before she paid for her gas and a bottle of pop. She went out and parked in the sleeper area before she read the rest.

The messages were all the same, basically. Each one got a tad terser, but she decided to wait until she'd rested before calling him. She had no doubt that he'd talked to Austin, and had his own opinion about what she should do. CJ tossed her phone on the shelf above her head and settled back to think.

Men sucked. CJ knew that was a bit immature, but she wasn't feeling very adult right now. The nerve of him telling her to sell her bar and get rid of her rig. She'd made a lot of money off of the latter, and was going to off the bar when she got it up and running. CJ reached for her phone when it vibrated. Unknown again. It was tempting to let it go to voicemail, but she thought it was full. Answering it, she was fully prepared to hang up on Phil or Austin if it was them.

"Miss Webber? It's Wayne Solomon of Solomon Trucking. I got your name from Preston Xpress. Brice Preston said you were looking to carry a few loads over the holiday season for him, and I was wondering if you could help us out with his deliveries?"

CJ sat up on her bed and moved to her passenger seat up front. "Yes, yes, I can. You want help with the Preston company moving freight? But you should know I have my own rig. I won't drive someone else's. If that's a problem, the—"

"No, no, that's not a problem. It's a blessing, as a matter of fact. We have two out now, rigs and men. They took to the Upper Canada and haven't been able to return yet…snow, don't you know. I have a load that needs to be in California…well, it should be there by Friday. I know it's short, but the receiver is willing to give you 'til Monday if you can, don't you know."

Friday. This was Thursday, and she was getting only an extra three days, maybe. She could do it, she supposed, but…. "Can you squeeze me until Wednesday late? I can do it then depending on where I pick up."

"Sure, and I'll be asking. You just give me a shake and a wiggle here and I'll ask." CJ had no clue what a "shake and wiggle" timeframe was, but waited all the same. Apparently, it wasn't long because Wayne was right back. "He said he can do that. Needs it, don't you know. The load is there, in your town at the railway. You get yourself to a faxamachine and I'll send it right over."

"Let me give you the email address I use. It's easier." While she rattled it off, she noticed a group of men behind a Preston Xpress trailer. She watched them for a minute before she realized they were looking sort of suspicious.

There were four of them and one of them was on what looked like a phone. He looked like he was writing something down when one of the other men produced a set of large bolt cutters. When he used them at the doors of the trailer where a seal or lock would be to prevent tampering of a load, she sat back in her seat. When the notice went off that she had an email, she nearly shot through the roof. Looking down at the bill of lading that Solomon had just sent her and then back at the trailer number just down from her, she groaned.

"Mother fuck, they match."

CHAPTER NINE

Dallas watched his brother pace. He would have laughed at Austin, but was afraid he'd hit him again. Dallas rubbed his jaw, thinking it had been worth it. He grinned when he thought of the dig he'd been able to give his brother about CJ.

"Where the hell could she be? Nobody could just disappear off the face of the earth like that. Especially in a rig that size." Dallas didn't point out that she wasn't the only rig on the road, and he was reasonably sure she could and had done just that.

"Have you talked to her friend the vamp lately? Maybe he knows something," Dallas asked instead. He grinned at his mother when she entered the kitchen.

"Phil told him if he called again, he'd tell CJ never to come back." She winked at Dallas. "Austin has made a nuisance of himself."

"I've done nothing of the sort," Austin practically snarled at them. One look from their mom made him change that quickly enough. "She ran off while I was on the phone with Mom. What possessed her to do that is beyond—"

"Oh for pity's sake, Austin, you were nearly foaming at the mouth when you came to the phone. Small wonder she didn't murder you instead of only leaving you." Dallas looked at his mom as she continued. "You should have heard him. He was screaming at her to come back and listen to him."

Dallas laughed. "So you what…told her that you loved her and she didn't like that idea? I thought you had a bit more style than that, big brother."

"I don't love her. I never said anything about love…ever. But she's my mate, and she will do as she's told." Dallas stared at Austin as he continued along that vein. "If I have to be saddled with someone like her then she'll learn her place. I don't have a great deal of time to go chasing her all over the place. She'll learn her place by my side or else."

"You're serious. Christ, what the hell is wrong with you? You expect her to simply shut up and mind like she's ten? No wonder she left you." Dallas stood up. "She's been gone for over eight hours. I, for one, hope she finds a hole and never comes up where you ever find her."

"She's my mate, and I will—"

"Lose her," their mother finished for Austin. "I never thought I'd hear those words from your mouth. That poor girl."

Whatever Austin was going to say to that was cut off when Dallas heard his cell phone ring. The tone told him it was pack business; the timing told him it was going to be bad. He was thrilled for the interruption…otherwise he would have probably murdered his brother. He answered with a bark of his name.

Silence greeted him, then a voice and a string of curse words that would have made most of the criminals he knew blush. Waiting for the tirade to finish, he smiled when the voice on the other end practically snarled at him. Oh, he was going to love this.

~~~

"I was told to use this phone to call the…I forget what he called you. The enforcer maybe?"

"Yes. That would be me. Who would have given you this number, and what is your name?" Dallas thought he already knew, but wanted to make sure.

"CJ Webber. I don't suppose you're a different Dallas, and one not related to Austin Force, are you? I mean, that would be just too good to be true."

He laughed at the hope in her voice. "You'd be wrong. I am. And you didn't answer my question."

"Isaac Dorsey handed me his phone to wait for you to answer. He claims you know him and because of the...situation I'm in and the help he's going to give me, he said you had to be informed. This is another wolf thing, isn't it?"

He looked over at his brother, who had stopped pacing to wait. Austin had to be involved if it was pack business, and Isaac was a member of their pack. He tightened his grip on the phone and hoped he could clear this up without Austin being aware of who he was talking to.

"Yes, it is. Tell me what's going on and I'll see what I can do. Isaac is a member of our pack and a detective. I know he's been working undercover for something. Does this involve any of that?" He closed his eyes when she answered yes. "I see. Tell me where you are and we'll be right there."

~~~

CJ handed the phone back to Isaac and walked back to her rig. Of all the people in the entire truck stop for her to see that she trusted, it would turn out to be another wolf. She climbed into the driver's seat and waited for Dallas and she had no doubt, Austin.

She climbed in and sat back on the plush seat. *Damn, damn, damn.* She thought about her mad dash to get as far away from the truck as possible while trying to figure out what to do about it. *Now look,* she thought, *up the creek and no paddle, but plenty of dogs...sorry,* she amended, *wolves.*

She'd moved her rig to the very back of the lot. She had been about that far back anyway when she parked in the first place, but had started up and was in the process of pulling into a space when she saw Isaac. She waved at him then pulled in two rigs down from him, and had just settled in again when he knocked at her door.

"Hey, kiddo. I'd heard you'd given up the road. Glad to see you...what's wrong?" She thought it strange that he sniffed her before he continued. "You smell...well, well. Who's the new guy?"

She flushed. There was no new guy, not even an old guy, she wanted to scream, but decided that a change of subject was better. She told him what she'd found out about Solomon Trucking instead of answering. In hindsight, she wished she'd just answered the guy's question.

"You saw them cut the seal? Who did it, do you know? Where is it now...the truck I, mean? Can you take me to it?" She stared at him, thinking, when he grinned. "I know you know about my kind now, so I figure you can be trusted."

"Your kind? What...I don't understand what you mean. And I'm not having anything to do with that company. I've got enough problems right now without buying more of my own." She started to close the door again before he or she said something stupid. It turned out he said something that pissed her off more than Austin had. Fucking dogs.

"I'm an undercover cop, and I'm investigating the theft of loads being taken off this and other lots all over the state. If you don't help me, CJ, I'll have to assume you're a part of the ring doing it and have you arrested. Help me and I'll owe you."

She looked down at him from her rig. "You said 'your kind.' What did you mean?" She was afraid she already knew the answer, but not how he knew.

"You've been marked by a wolf—a werewolf. Powerful one by the scent. And he would have had to tell you or the scent wouldn't be so strong. A wolf can't mark someone like that unless he's found his mate. Are you his mate?"

"Mark? Mark how? I...he didn't bite me. I told him...fuck!" Dawning was slow in coming to her. "You're a dog...er, wolf too?"

His grin made her feel like she was stupid. "Very good...yes, I am. And he's marked you by...well, he would have...shit, girl. He had sex with you. His essences, his...hum...his semen, would be enough to keep other wolves at bay that weren't already mated."

His semen. His cum. He had come on her and— "He didn't have sex with me. He just came on me." Isaac was nodding before she finished. "He marked me. I'm going to kill him. I'm going to buy a gun...and why are you shaking your head no?"

"You can't hurt him. I mean, you can try, but because you're his mate, you won't be able to cause him harm. Mates are a little rough during sex, so something about the DNA makes it so that they can't get too rough and really hurt the other." Isaac smiled at her. "Didn't he explain any of this to you before you left him?"

She didn't answer. She was trying to absorb the fact that Isaac said that she and Austin were mates. What the hell did that mean, she wondered? She didn't think she could take much more, so she changed the subject back to Solomon.

"I not only saw them cut the seal, but they want me to take the load for them. I haven't told them no yet, but...there you go again. Why are you shaking your head 'no' this time?" She just wanted to sit down or lie down. Right now, she wanted to hide, then lie down.

"You've just given us the break we need, darlin'. And if I have my way, you and me, we're going traveling

79

together. Solomon has been screwing over his pack for months, and with you seeing and then being invited to play, why, I got it as good as solved."

"You take it then. I'm going to go and find me a nice company to work for and become another driver for the rest of my life. I so don't need this shit." She leaned back against the truck as what he'd just said sank in. "He's a wolf too? Christ almighty, isn't anyone who they claim to be?"

Isaac called his boss. Not the furry one, he told her, but the one that he worked for. The guy showed up ten minutes later, and she repeated what she'd seen. Then she'd shown them the BOL she'd gotten from Solomon.

"This is great," Detective Leo Weaver told her. "Not only do we have the goods, and a driver who is gonna help us, but because you were nice enough to have him email it to you, we got his IP address too."

She didn't care about the Internet Protocol address, the string of numbers responsible for routing packets of information across network boundaries; she was more concerned with him thinking she was going to help them. But every time she tried to point out she wasn't going to accept the load, both men would literally pat her on the head and go on as though she hadn't spoken. When Isaac asked her if she'd wait on the line for this enforcer person, she decided that he might be a better person to listen. Turns out she was wrong about that too, if he was anything like his asshole brother.

And now here she sat, waiting. She wasn't sure how to tell Leo she wasn't going to drive the rig. She wasn't sure what to tell Austin or his brother. Hell, she thought, she wasn't even sure what they had to do with any of this. She was still trying to figure it out when she heard her door open.

"Go away. I said I'm not taking this load, and you can stick your threat up your ass for all I care." She heard someone snort and closed her eyes. "Please tell me you're Isaac."

"It's Austin. And you're damn right in thinking you're not taking this load. I'm not having my mate going across the county, much less across the country. Besides, we have a few more things to discuss, and you're not leaving until we do."

If he thought telling her he agreed with her about the load and her not taking it would work then he was wrong. She would take it now even if it meant certain death for her. She rolled to her side and looked up at him. He looked even more furious with her now than he had before. She lay back down without speaking.

Another knock at her door made her sit up, but she didn't leave the sleeper. Austin's brother sat in the other seat. She lay back down on the bed without speaking to either of them. They, however, had plenty to say.

"She's not going on the run. She is finally being smart for once," Austin said. CJ wanted to hit him, but decided he'd be pissed enough when she drove off. She had to smile at that thought.

"Austin, has anyone ever told you you're a prick? Besides me, I mean. Christ, the woman is right there." CJ thought she might like this brother. She listened to him when he continued. "You should really learn to say please and thank you."

"She had already decided to not go, so what would be the point? I'm taking her home, and we'll get our differences settled and this mate thing complete. She'll whelp soon, and everything will be normal again." CJ snorted and Austin turned to her. "You have something to add?"

The knock at the door prevented her from answering. She sat up again when Isaac yelled for her. "Kid? You in here?"

"Yeah. You need me again?" She moved to the doorway from the sleeping compartment and then out the door on Dallas's side. She heard him chuckle and a growl. She didn't even bother looking at either man. She purposely shut the door when she got out and walked away with Isaac.

"So," he said in a low voice. "You have an alpha as a mate. Good for you. I hear that Austin is a good guy."

She wanted to scream. "Then you mate with him. He doesn't want me anyway." She fell in step with him as they moved across the lot toward the other detective. "He only wants me because I can 'whelp,' or some other shit."

Isaac did a little stutter step then continued on. He looked at her oddly, but didn't comment on what she'd said. She knew he would, but right now he seemed to be mulling things over.

"Miss Webber, I'm going to have to insist that you take this load for us. There are millions of—" She cut Leo off.

"I'm going. I'll take it. Just tell me what I need to do and I can get going. I only have a few days to get across the country and I need to get going. Oh, and you're paying for the gas. I do this on my terms and not—"

"I told you no. You're not going anywhere." She closed her eyes at Austin's loud voice. "You are going home with me, CJ, and that's final."

"Miss Webber, you really need to take this. We could take your truck from you, but I'd rather not. It's been established that you are the driver. Now, I've set it up with Isaac to be your second driver. And he'll—"

The deep feral growl had all three of them turning. Austin was looking at Isaac as if he was going to hurt him. CJ stepped in front of her friend and felt his arms on her shoulders the next instant.

"CJ, don't. You'll only make him madder if you try and protect me," Isaac whispered near her ear. "Step away from me and I'll settle this with your mate."

"He's not my fucking mate," she shouted. "Christ, I wish you people would stop calling me that. I. Am. Not. His. Mate. I'm going alone or with you. I'm so fucking sick of this." She turned back to her truck and started stalking toward it. If one person said the word "mate" to her again, she was going to kill them all. She got into the rig just as Austin came up beside it. She hit the locks and started the thing up before she realized Dallas still sat in the passenger seat.

"You going to California with me? If not, then get the hell out." She was doing a quick check of all the stuff she needed when he spoke.

"I'm not going, but thanks for asking." He didn't move, but stared at his brother. "This isn't the way to handle him. You're only going to make him madder."

Of course she didn't answer, but continued with what she was doing. Like she gave a shit what his temper was like. CJ was just pushing in the clutch to shift into drive when Dallas put his hand over hers. She looked up at him. "Get out," she said. It was all she could manage if she didn't want to go screaming into the night. "Just get out."

He seemed to know she was close to losing it, so he nodded and put his hand on the handle. He turned back to her before he got out. "I like you Charlie Jane. Very much so, as a matter of fact. I'm going to enjoy watching the two of you come to terms with this. Because you will have to eventually." With that, he got out. Before she could move on, Austin got in.

Without a word, she put it in first gear and moved to the line of trucks where the Preston truck was sitting. She thought if he wanted to come with her, she'd not speak to him.

CHAPTER TEN

Austin watched her drive the big semi up the lane. He had an idea what was going on, but didn't get all the details before she stormed off in the direction of the rig. Isaac had said he was going with her so that he could drive part of the way, but Austin told him that wasn't happening. The older man seemed to think that was funny, but Austin failed to see the humor in it.

He watched her back up to the trailer. She did it with ease and expertise. Austin was impressed with the way she seemed to just know when to stop without hitting the trailer, and when she grabbed a pair of heavy gloves and got out, he wasn't sure if he should follow. He was sort of afraid she meant to leave him, and he wasn't going to let that happen.

She was standing on the back of her rig hooking up some wires when he came around to where she was. It looked like she was putting in the electrical harness from the trailer to the rig she was driving. When she hopped down instead of waiting for him to help her, he knew that he was going to have a long ride ahead of him.

"Here, let me do that." Austin tried to move her out of the way so that he could wind the heavy looking bar that she was moving. A sharp growl from her made him step back. She finished the job ten minutes later.

The bar she had been turning seemed to lift the large leg-like things just under the front of the trailer. He was amazed that when she finished hooking the trailer to the rig, it had been so seamless; trailer standing alone, to semi and trailer as one. When she went to the back of the trailer and practically stepped under it to do something, he nearly grabbed her and pulled her out but she was back out from under it a minute later. She did the same to the other side. When she got back in the truck, he hurried to the other side and climbed in. He watched as she moved the truck back until he felt something slam into them from the rear. He looked out the mirror in time to see Isaac moving to the side he was on and knocking on the door.

"Here you go, kid. There's over two grand in there for gas and food." She took the envelope from him. "Your tandems are back and your lights all work. There will be another five grand when you get to the drop." He handed her a bag. "There's a cell in there and also a list of phone numbers. Leo or I will call you every two to see where you are. You are gonna see a bunch of cops, but you won't be stopped. They are on the watch for you. Got it all?"

She nodded, but Austin had questions. "Where are we going, and who will be watching over her in the mean time? Where will we be staying and how will we get back?"

Isaac just grinned and shut the door. Austin felt the truck lurch forward, and they were suddenly moving toward the highway.

Austin thought he'd give her a little while to calm down before he talked to her. He knew they were going to California and that the load they were taking was stolen. What he didn't know was why she had been chosen and why she had disobeyed him. He'd nearly broken his promise to himself by starting to ask her some of his questions when a ringing sound startled him. She reached over her head and turned something. Suddenly, there was another voice in the truck with them.

"Hey, CJ, I have some news on that property you asked me about. Is it okay to talk or have you left yet?"

Austin recognized Phil's voice. He looked over at CJ when she answered. He wasn't thrilled at being ignored, but he might find out something if he let her hang herself.

"I have a passenger. But as I could care less what he does or thinks, go ahead. Was it as good as I said it would be?"

There was a bark of laughter then Phil spoke. "Hello, Austin. I didn't know you drove a rig."

"I don't. I'm along because she doesn't have the sense to learn to listen to what she's been told. I needed to drop everything I was doing to make sure she didn't get into any more trouble before I could claim her."

He knew the moment he said it he'd hurt her. And he knew from the silence on the other end of the phone, Phil knew it too. Before he could say anything—not that he knew what to say—CJ spoke again.

"Did you get it? The property, I mean? And please tell me you got a good price." Some of the enthusiasm had gone out of her voice, Austin noticed. "I want it, but not for much over what I said to offer."

"I got it for twenty percent less than you offered. They were just glad to get rid of it." Papers rattled around as Phil continued. "The closing is on January tenth. I figured you could work around that."

She glanced his way before answering. "Sure, that'll be fine. Set up the rest of the...you can set up the other stuff on the same day, right?"

"Sure," Phil answered. "It's already done. And the rest of it starts as soon as the ground thaws. I have the trust set up the way you said. The mayor wants to be there, of course. I have a few people lined up already to start the hiring process. I figured maybe thirty to start."

"Yeah, okay." Another glance at Austin before she continued. "We'll talk more later, okay? I think…it's too much over the phone."

They talked for a few more minutes before they disconnected. Austin wanted to know what was going on that involved ground thawing and trust funds, but figured she wouldn't tell him even if he asked. He stared out the window and realized they were turning into a Walmart. As they parked, she explained.

"I need supplies. You can come or not, I could care less." She got out and left him there. She was walking to the entrance when he caught up with her. He grabbed her arm to stop her when she stalked past him.

"You have no right to be pissed at me. You brought this all on yourself."

She didn't say anything, but jerked free and walked inside.

He needed clothes if they were going to California and back in a truck. He didn't have a clue how long that would take, but figured it would be at least a week. But he didn't trust that she wouldn't leave him either, so he asked her for the keys to the truck.

He wasn't sure she'd give them to him, but when she reached into her pocket and handed them to him without a word, he didn't feel any better about himself. If she planned to not speak to him for the entire trip, it was going to be a very long one.

Grabbing up several pairs of jeans, underwear, and socks, he was standing in the shirts area when his phone rang. He wasn't sure what Dallas wanted, but knew it couldn't be good.

"I have some information on Isaac. He's on an undercover project with the Feds to find out about a ring of thefts of trailers over the past few months. Mostly it's been liquor and cigarettes, but some of the merchandise has been high end electronics."

"How did CJ get involved then?" Austin grabbed up three packages of shirts and then went to find some heavier shirts while he waited for his brother to answer.

"Wrong place at the wrong time mostly. She put out the word that she was looking to make some hauls, and for whatever reason, ended up in the truck stop here to see Solomon and his crew cut a seal off a load."

Isaac had explained what a seal was. It was a plastic strip that secured the back of the trailer doors when transporting merchandise. It didn't prevent anyone from breaking in...it was just a way for the destination where the load was going to ensure that the load or merchandise hadn't been tampered with. The seal was stamped with a number or code that matched paperwork for the company to compare with. A load with the wrong seal number was generally turned away.

"And she knew Isaac and confessed all to him? Why didn't she go to the police? Why him?" Dallas laughed and Austin knew he wasn't going to like the answer.

"He said he saw her parking and went to say hello. He said he smelled that she'd been marked and congratulated her on it. He said he felt like her dad explaining just how you marked her and what it meant." Dallas sobered a bit before the final bomb was dropped. "Mom isn't happy about that either. She's really pissed at you right now. It's probably a good thing you'll be gone a while."

Austin was standing in Health and Beauty when he saw CJ going toward the ladies' department. Her cart was full—bottled water, canned goods, apples, paper plates, and other sundry filled most of it, along with some clothes that he couldn't identify. He wondered if he should offer to pay at least half and decided she wouldn't take it, but he'd see that she got it.

"Tell her that I'm sorry and I didn't mean for her to find out that way." Austin threw a deodorant and some liquid soap in his cart before heading to the front to check out. He was walking by the pregnancy tests when he looked up at CJ again. "Dallas, can you look into something for me? I would like to know what CJ is setting up with a trust fund. The closing is January tenth."

Austin told him everything he'd heard before his brother asked why he didn't just ask her himself. "She's not speaking to me," was his reply.

After hanging up, Austin threw a box of condoms in the cart. He wasn't sure where he'd left the ones Dallas had given him and if he was honest with himself, he wasn't sure if he wanted his brother's. Austin went to check out and tried not to think about why he was buying them.

~~~

CJ had managed to cram all her stuff into one cart. She usually had most of these items with her, but with another person and a long haul, she didn't want to stop and refill. She was going to be cutting it close anyway. By the time she got to the truck, Austin was already there. She ignored his offer to help her load it in the truck, and put it all on her seat to stash away when she got in the sleeper.

Everything in the sleeper part of the cab was bolted down. What wasn't bolted was in things that she could close off or in most cases, stash into stuff. She looked around at the area.

There was no floor. The bed took up most of that bit of the space. She had decided that a larger bed superseded a twin because she wanted comfort, not standing room. She had a microwave that worked off its own battery, a small refrigerator, and also a hot plate. The television was a nineteen-incher with a DVD player under it. She had some movies, but seldom watched anything but the news when she could get Internet service.

She had a set of drawers under the bed and emptied one of them for her rider. She also moved a few of her hanging things in the small closet. The food went in the bottom of the closet, and the bottled water went between the seats in the small electric cooler she kept there for it. She was wadding up the bags and putting them in the drawer when she heard the door slam.

CJ didn't speak to him when she got in the driver's seat. She had to work on how much he needed to know. She started the truck and looked over at him as he buckled in.

"I don't want you here, but since you are, you're on my turf. My rig, my rules. I drive for twelve and sleep eight. I don't have time to stop when you get a whim, so if you have to take a break, tough. I have less than five days to get across the country. There's food and water if you want it. If not, then you'll starve. When I stop for gas, you can shower or whatever, I don't care. I use what they offer and I won't, contrary to what you think, leave you stranded." She put the truck in gear and looked back at him. "Oh yeah, I sleep alone."

They were getting on the highway when he finally spoke. She was actually surprised he'd waiting that long. She was sure she'd pissed him off, but frankly, didn't care.

"May I speak, or is that against your rules too?" She shrugged her reply. "All right. I would like to pay for whatever half of the stuff you bought costs. I know you got money from Isaac, but that is for you, not me."

"No. I don't want anything from you." She looked down at the speedometer and decided if she could maintain this speed for the next few hours, she could make St. Louis, Missouri by the time she needed some sleep.

"CJ, I have to insist that you—"

"Insist all you want. I'm not taking anything from you. Now, if you don't have any other pressing matters, I'd appreciate it if you shut the hell up. I have over four hundred miles to eat today before I can stop for the night."

Austin sat there for another hour and for the most part, didn't say anything. He had several calls, but she ignored them and concentrated on the road. This trip might have come at a good time, but with him there, it wasn't going well. When he got up and went to the sleeper, she sighed. This was going to be a really long trip.

By the time she pulled into the truck stop on I-44 West, she was both exhausted and starving. Deciding she could use a hot meal and a shower, she turned to tell him what she was doing and he came through the door.

"Showers cost about five bucks. I suggest you get one here. Tomorrow I'm going a bit further, about five hundred miles and with only a couple of stops. I'm getting a shower and dinner." She got out before he could comment.

The shower was stingy with its spray and hot water, but it felt good. She dressed in her sweats so that when she ate she could just go back to the rig and climb into bed. She didn't care what he did tonight...she just hoped that he stayed out of her way. By the time she was dried and dressed, she felt she could almost eat a horse, and she hated that she felt a little disappointed when Austin wasn't in the diner when she came out.

She was just looking over the menu when her phone rang. Smiling for the first time in hours, she answered. Phil had been her friend too long for her to stay mad for very long.

"Hey, buddy. What's going on? Please tell me that there is nothing wrong with the buy. I need that area to finish the project." She noticed the silence and knew something more had happened. "What it is? Are you all right?"

"I'm sorry, honey, but I have terrible news. There was an explosion from a gas leak in the basement of the Jewel. Everything was a total loss. The explosion was felt for about ten miles. The fire department said had you been there, you would never have made it out."

She felt the room tilt. She hadn't lived there long, not even long enough to have moved her stuff from storage into it, but it had been her first real place. She laid her head on the table top and tried to think.

"Did anyone get hurt? I mean, windows breaking or anything? Tell everyone I'll pay for any damages. Phil…."

"It's all right. No one was hurt. There were a few windows broken in a couple of houses just down the road, but since the Jewel was so far out, there wasn't as much damage as there could have been if it had been in town. The insurance paid up. I kept it up since you inherited it. Your car…it's gone too, I'm afraid."

"I don't really care about all that. Just make sure…make sure that no one was hurt. Make some sort of restitution to the fire department. I don't know…don't they have a Christmas fund or something?" Her mind raced over what to do. "Make sure that everyone's windows are repaired too."

"I've already done that. I'll make arrangements for money to be sent to the toy drives they are having this weekend. I'm assuming you want it to be anonymous, correct?" She told him yes and could hear him scribbling as he spoke. "The Red Cross too. I'll make sure I send them a donation as well."

After clearing a few more things off the list he always did, he asked her about her run. "It's okay. Austin watched some movies, I suppose. I'm sitting in the truck stop on I-forty-four."

"You take care, you hear me? And call me if you need anything. I love you, kiddo."

"Love you too." CJ looked up when someone sat down. She raised her head when Austin sat next to her, his hair still damp. She closed her phone just as the waitress came to the table.

CHAPTER ELEVEN

Something had happened. Austin wasn't sure what, but she wasn't even rising to the bait when he tried to piss her off. When her dinner came, all she did was move the fries around and nibble at the burger.

He'd asked her twice, and both times all he got was a "nothing" from her. He was about to call Phil when Austin noticed that someone was walking toward the table. CJ groaned and put the fakest smile he'd ever seen on her face.

"Well, as I live and breathe, if it isn't Charlie Jane Webber. How you doing, darlin'? Still driving, I guess." The man looked over at Austin and put out his hand. "I'm Dudley Cantrell. I own Cantrell Shipping Express. Been trying to get little Charlie Jane to join my stable of drivers for near about five years. Always turns me down."

"Because I don't like you. Don't you have some other person to annoy? I'm eating and don't want to puke on that fine fake suit of yours." Austin nearly bit his tongue off trying not to laugh at the man's face when CJ made her statement. "Go away, Dudley."

"See how she is?" Dudley asked of Austin. "No matter how badly she treats me, I still want her to work for me. What will it take, Charlie Jane? Hmm? You have to have a price."

"She said to get the hell away from her," a deep voice said just behind Austin. "I would suggest you move along, or I might have to show you how I treat men I just don't like."

Dudley, who had just pulled out a chair to sit, backed up. "Now, Faith, there isn't any reason for you to get all heed up. I was only having a nice conversation with her. Tell her, Charlie Jane. Tell Faith we was having a nice conversation."

"He was just leaving. Bye, Dudley. Oh and by the way, it's CJ, not Charlie Jane." CJ smiled at Dudley, and not a nice one either. "If you bother me again, I'll have my friend drain you."

Dudley backed up quickly after that and nearly fell twice trying to get away. Austin watched his progress, but was distracted by the woman.... Faith, he presumed, sat down in the chair next to him. He couldn't help but stare at her.

Even sitting down, she was huge. Not fat really, though she did have a few pounds on her frame. But she was tall. Austin was six-foot-four, and she would have towered over him by another foot. Her figure was...full, he supposed, with a large chest and generous hips. He would have bet she weighed close to four hundred pounds. When she settled in the chair, Austin was sure he heard the chair scream for mercy. He looked down at the hand she extended to him and wondered briefly if she could crush his.

"You sure are a pretty thing, aren't you? I'm Faith McKenzie. I own this here joint." Austin shook her hand and was surprised by the gentleness of her grip. "You Miss CJ's partner?"

"No, he's not. He's just along for the ride." Austin glanced over at CJ when she kicked him under the table. "He is just enjoying the scenery."

Faith threw back her head and laughed. "Oh, honey, he's sniffing around for a piece of that scenery too."

Austin laughed. He liked this woman and her brash, blunt way. "I'm Austin Force. It's a nice establishment you have here. The food was excellent."

"Thanks. My husband cooks, though there are days when I try my hand." They both looked at CJ when she snorted. "You think I can't cook, girl?"

"I know you can't. If you remember correctly, I was here last time you tried your hand at cooking. I think eighteen people died, and twelve more threatened to sue." The twinkle in CJ's eye made his breath catch while she continued teasing the older woman. "Then there were the small animals that died from the fumes coming from the dumpster."

Austin couldn't believe how beautiful she was when she smiled like she was. He realized in that moment that he'd never seen her smile until that moment. As she and Faith continued to tease one another, Austin watched her. She was having fun and laughing, so that for a few minutes, whatever had been bothering her when he sat down was forgotten.

"I have some stuff for you," CJ said after a good belly laugh. "I was going to send it tomorrow, but when I found out I'd be coming this way...well, I decided to bring it."

She moved a white envelope across the table toward Faith, who took it and put it down her shirt. Faith nodded before she spoke.

"You know more and more need this nowadays. You been real helpful to some of them. Cleo and me, we got a list of some who could use it. We even have some of our own to put in this year." Faith wiped away a tear. "I don't know where me and Cleo'd be without your help all those years ago."

"Never mind that. You know to...you know. Keep it quiet. I don't want...you just say whatever you did before." CJ seemed embarrassed and gathered up her bag and coat.

"I gotta get some sleep. You keep out of the kitchen while I'm gone."

With a quick kiss on Faith's cheek, CJ grabbed up the check and seemed to race toward the cashier. She was out the door before Austin realized she'd taken his check too. He looked over at Faith, who was staring intently at him.

"She know what you are? CJ, she know you're a wolf?"

Austin leaned back in the chair and regarded the woman in front of him. "Yes. You're not a supernatural, so how did you know?" He looked over when she did when a short, balding man came toward them.

"My husband. Cleo McKenzie, this is Austin Force. Austin was just asking me how I knew he was a canine."

The man took CJ's seat and smiled before answering. "Our dishwasher smelled you. He's a were, though not wolf. He's a cat...panther, I believe. Told us you were here and sitting with your mate. Imagine our surprise when he pointed to our CJ's table."

Austin wondered if CJ knew her friends knew of his kind, and decided almost immediately that she didn't. Otherwise, she would have taken his and Phil's news a little better. Austin wondered how well these people knew CJ. Before he could ask, Faith shook her head.

"Don't ask. I won't tell you anyway, but don't ask. You want to know what she's about then you'll have to get it from her." Faith shifted on the chair before continuing. "She's something else, our CJ. And I'll be honest with you when I tell you we don't know much about her either. She's a...what did you call her, honey?" Faith turned to her husband as she asked.

"Enigma, a puzzle of sorts. Can't figure her out either. 'Bout the time we get her where we think we know, she changes into something more."

Austin could see that. She was driving him crazy too. He nodded toward where Dudley had gone. "That man, has he hurt her? Tried to do anything that would have him killed?"

Cleo laughed before answering. "About six months ago, she came in for dinner. I think it was right after her rat bastard of a father died. Me and the missus was away on a second honeymoon or he'd a not gotten to the table. But CJ, she took care of him. He was getting too close and she...well, it's said that he doesn't sit for too long a period of time no more."

Austin looked over at Faith as she picked up the story. "She threw knives at him. Hit his ass about a dozen times with our steak knives before she let him get away." She nodded to a frame on the wall and Austin burst out laughing.

There were a dozen black handled steak knives mounted on a board and framed. The caption under it said, "You fuck with ours, you get skewered."

Faith looked at Austin before she spoke, her voice low and full of meaning. "She doesn't think she needs anyone, or that anyone needs her. You'd do well to remember that."

Austin thought about that as he went back to her rig. Cleo was right, she was an enigma. He just wasn't sure yet if he wanted to figure her out. As he sat in the passenger seat and looked back at her sleeping in the big bed, he wondered about her.

She didn't really need him to take care of her. Austin thought that pissed him off more than he wanted to admit. CJ didn't seem to be the least bit intimidated by him either. He grinned when he thought of the knives hanging on the wall. His phone going off made her stir, and he grabbed it, whispered a quiet "hang on" to his brother, and got out of the rig.

"How is she doing? Poor girl," Dallas said when he told him she was asleep. "Sucks what happened, doesn't it? But she has you, right?"

Austin didn't answer. He didn't know what had happened because she hadn't told him. He couldn't even be mad because she hadn't. Austin leaned back against the cab and closed his eyes. He'd been a complete ass with her from the start. If he was smart, he'd call someone to come and get him or catch the next flight out and let her be.

"Austin," his brother asked. "She didn't tell you, did she? Damn it, Austin, either take her as your mate or fucking leave her alone. The girl has been through enough. Come home. When this is over, then you might start over with her."

"What happened?" Austin refused to acknowledge that his brother was probably correct. She was his, damn it.

"The Jewel blew up earlier today. Gas leak from a line that should have been closed off a decade or two ago. The fire marshal said that if anyone would have been inside, there would have been no way to escape. He said that the house went up in a fireball so quickly that it's small wonder more windows weren't broken out. As it was, there were houses about ten miles away that got a little kick back from it."

Icy sweat formed on Austin's body. She would have been there had she not been on this run. He sat down on the step and let the fact that she was asleep behind him wash over him.

"Was anyone hurt? And did she have insurance?" Austin didn't want to think about her being hurt. He also didn't want to think about why. "Tell whoever it is we'll take care of the damages."

"Too late. Phil had a crew already doing repairs before the fire department left the scene. He contracted some of our guys to do the work, paid them double to do it today. There were no reported injuries." His pause made Austin leery. "Then one of the pack members called a bit ago to let me know that a gift card came to them by courier. She sent everyone a five hundred dollar credit card for their inconvenience."

The fact that he would have done the same thing made him smile. She was something else. He stood up and looked at the door behind him before he spoke.

"I'm not coming home. I'm going to work this out. I've been…well, I've been a fool." He thought his brother snorted, but ignored it. "Work with Phil, get as much cleared away as you can before she gets back."

They talked for a few more minutes and then hung up. Austin climbed back into the rig and then back into the sleeper. It was do or die time. He needed her in his life whether she wanted it or not. Smiling, he thought it might be fun to see who came out on top.

~~~

CJ woke when she felt someone near. Looking around the semi-dark cab, she saw a shape and nearly cried out when Austin told her it was him. She rolled over on the bed and covered her head when he turned the light on.

"Go away. I have a long day tomorrow and I—hey!" She flipped back over when the covers were stripped off her. "What the fuck do you think you're doing?"

"I need to speak to you. Now." Austin started unbuttoning his shirt. "But first I'm going to shift, and I don't want you to freak out."

"I don't freak out, thank you very much. And shift your ass out on the seat. I'm too tired to fuck around tonight." She found herself watching mesmerized as he undid the buttons. "I want you to stop that right now."

"I have to stay as a wolf for at least an hour or it's too much on my system. Don't scream because we're too close to the other rigs for them not to hear you." When he pulled his shirt off and dropped it on the floor, he started on his belt. "I'm taking off my clothes because the shift will tear them up."

"Shift? I don't...you're thinking you're going to change into a wolf? Here? Now? Oh no you don't, buck-o. You just get that notion out of your head right now." She tried sitting up in the bed to get away from him, but he grabbed her leg. "Let me go, Austin. This isn't funny."

His belt hit the floor and he worked the snap and zipper with his free hand. She could see his cock hard against his briefs. She licked her suddenly dry lips and looked up at him when he groaned.

"I want you. I want to bury myself deep inside your pussy and fuck you. But you need to see this." He let go of her leg and pulled his pants free along with his boxers.

Before she could move, there was a tightening in the tiny room. Then he began to change. She watched as he stretched out his arms and they suddenly became furred. His hands began to morph and his fingers elongated. When he said her name, she looked at his face as it too began to change. His jaw lengthened and teeth began to fill the space left open. Then he was gone. In his place lay a black wolf. She scrambled back to the wall when it moved toward her.

"Stay," she commanded with her hand up. "Don't come any closer. I'll...I'll shoot you if you do."

He moved up the bed, crawling with his belly on the mattress. When he touched his nose to her foot, she jerked it close to her body. He lay there for several seconds before he began to crawl again. She was so crunched in the corner she could barely breathe.

His tongue lapped at her hand she had wrapped around her leg. She peeked at him and was surprised to see him sitting close to her, his tongue hanging out like a big, sappy dog.

"If I pet you, will I get to keep all my fingers?" He snorted at her question. At least she thought he did; either that or he sneezed.

Reaching out tentatively, she brushed her fingers over his chest fur. It was soft and warm. The need to bury her fingers in its depths made her look at his face. She watched for any sign that he would hurt her while she did as she wanted.

"I'm either really still asleep or there's a wolf in my bed." That caused her to laugh, but it sounded sort of maniacal even to her ears. "Okay, so you're a wolf. Now what?"

Austin, because she didn't know what else to call him, laid his huge head on her leg when she stretched out. She scratched him behind his ear and thought about all the shit she'd encountered over the past six months. Not sure he could understand her, she lifted his head up and looked him in the eye.

"Blink once if you understand me." His eyes closed and opened. "Well, that could have been a normal blink, now couldn't it? Let me see. Okay, if you understand me...lick my cheek, the right one."

He stared at her for so long she started to get up, but his big, wet tongue came out and soaked her right cheek. She couldn't move.

"I'm not freaking out, but you have to admit this is fucked up. I go my entire life as if nothing is out of the ordinary, and suddenly I know a pack of wolves and a vampire." She moved to the edge of the bed to think and he moved closer to her. "You need to back off. I can't think with you touching me like this."

He moved back to the other end of the bed and she looked at the doorway. She needed a walk. Needed to just go outside and come back in and things would be back to normal. When she moved toward the opening, the wolf growled deep in his throat. She sat down.

"I can't think. I was just going out.... Why am I explaining this to you? You're not real. I'm going to go outside and when I come back—"

She was suddenly lying on the bed and he was over her body. When she opened her mouth, his paw, a big fucking paw, came down on her face. She was reaching up to jerk it off when she heard someone outside the truck.

Whispering, she stayed still. "You heard them, didn't you? I don't suppose you can tell me who it is, can you? You know, friend or foe?"

She thought she felt him laugh; his belly, warm against her, sort of rumbled. Then the rattle of the door made her stiffen.

CJ could see that it was locked. She was worried about the other door, the driver's door, because from where she was, she couldn't see it. Whoever it was, she decided it was foe. If it had been friend, they would have called out. Both she and the wolf lay very still until Austin got off her, went to the front of the cab, and sat on the seat.

CHAPTER TWELVE

Austin sat there for the rest of the hour. He didn't want to leave her because he knew that, even if he could have gotten her to open the door, she'd follow him. She would think to protect him even now that he'd shifted for her. When he could shift back, he went back to the sleeper to find her sitting at the end of the bed with her gun in her hand. Austin didn't waste any time shifting back this time, but let it come over him quickly.

"You were faster coming back." The calmness in her voice scared him. "Are you going to get dressed?"

"Do you want me to?" His voice was low and arousal made it deep. She couldn't stop staring at his cock. "I told you before I want to fuck you. That hasn't changed."

His body was on fire. He could see her nipples, hard peaks, brush against her undershirt. She had her hands fisted into the sheets so she wouldn't reach out and touch him, he thought. When he wrapped his hand around his cock for her, she moaned.

"I can smell you, Charlie. Smell your body's need, your arousal." He took a step toward her as he continued. "I want to taste you. Lick your juices from your pussy and drink your cum. Would you like to come in my mouth, on my tongue?"

Yes, she would, he could tell. When he was standing over her, his cock a few inches from her, she licked her lips. His cock jerked in his hand. He needed to be inside her now.

"Lie back. I want to eat you." She didn't disobey him, but did just as he commanded. Austin dropped to the floor on his knees and touched her calves. She jerked at his touch.

"Easy, love. I'm not going to hurt you." He pulled her to the edge of the bed, her legs hanging off as he moved between them. "You smell delicious. Are you wet for me, Charlie?"

Austin moved his fingers along her panties. He wasn't surprised to find them soaked. Her thighs were also wet. When she tried to bring her legs together, he slid his finger under the elastic and entered her.

"Austin, please," she begged. "You don't want to do this. You want…you want to…."

Moving his finger in and out of her, he could feel how tight she was. "I want to eat you until you come over and over. Christ, you're so wet. I'm going to get my fill of you. But these have to go."

Removing his finger from her sheath, she whimpered, and when he curled his hands in the tiny strips of ribbon on either side of her hips, she started panting. Her breath was heating his skin and he had hardly touched her. Before he tore her panties off, he wanted to see the rest of her.

"Take off the shirt," he commanded harshly. "Take it off so I can see your breasts. I want to see them tighten when you come."

She stared at him for several seconds. He could see the glazed look of need in her eyes. After barking at her again to take it off, she lifted it over her head and dropped it on the floor beside his discarded clothes.

When he ripped her panties from her body, her breasts jerked. His beast snarled at him to bite, to sink his canines deep into the soft flesh and mark her. Trying to calm the wolf, he shifted on his knees and buried his nose deep in her pussy.

He had tasted her before, but she wasn't fighting him this time. Her body wanted his…the cream gushing from her pussy told him that. He lapped his tongue from gate to clit and was dizzy from the taste of her. Taking her hard nubbin into his mouth, he sucked hard and entered her again with his finger.

Christ, she was tight. Her channel milked at his finger, pulling him deeper with every thrust. Using his free hand, he lifted her up until she was a feast before him. Pushing his tongue into her pussy, he gathered her cream and tasted her. Even as he slid another, then another finger into her, she filled him. Her bud, ripe for him, beckoned his mouth. Taking her clit into his mouth again, he nipped her and she shattered.

Austin knew he wasn't going to last. He wanted her with a desperation he'd never felt before. Standing over her, he looked down at her even as her body continued to spasm and jerk. A fine dew of sweat covered her, and he thought if he lived another three lifetimes he'd never see anything more beautiful. Reaching toward the shelf above her head for a condom, not wanting her to refuse him now, he tore the package open even as his wolf snarled for release.

"Take me. Now. I want you to take me now." Her breathless plea nearly felled him. He held the rolled condom in his hand. "Now, Austin, take me please. I want to feel you inside of me when you come."

"I won't last. Not long, I won't last. And my wolf…he needs to take his bite. He needs to mark you." He would take her whether she wanted the wolf or not, but he wouldn't bite her unless she said yes. And he also needed her to understand she'd be his. "The bite, it will mark you. No one will touch you. No one will live if they do."

She nodded. "Yes. I beg of you, take me."

He felt the wolf snarl at him and move along his skin. He knew what she was seeing, the change, the shift. His canines sharpened in his mouth and he snarled at her. Coming down onto her, he entered her hard and fast, then stilled when she cried out.

A virgin…Charlie was a virgin. He calmed then, held himself up on his elbows, and looked down at her. Tears ran down her cheeks and using his thumb, he brushed them way.

"You should have told me. I would have…I would have tried to take more care with you."

She looked up at him.

"I don't…do you no longer want me?"

Austin burst out laughing. It came from deep within him and startled him. "No. I want you. Now more than ever." He brushed another tear away. "Did I hurt you?"

"Yes. No. I don't…you're very full in me. I didn't even have time to wonder if you'd fit. You didn't, did you? I'm sorry. Maybe if I move—" She moaned when she shifted her hips. When she did it again, her eyes widened and her mouth opened. "Austin, can you…will you move? Please?"

He slid out of her tightness only to move back slowly. He could feel the sweat move down his spine, the effort to not hurt her killing him slowly. But the look on her face, the look that told him she was enjoying this, made him want to see to her pleasure over his.

"Wrap your legs around my hips. That's it." He groaned when she did as he asked. Reaching down, he cupped her breast and nibbled just on the tip.

Moving slowly, he felt her body responding to his. Her fingers dug into his shoulders and then moved down his back to his ass. Her nails dug deep. He needed to slow her down or he was going to come before she did. Rolling to his back, he brought her with him so that she now spread over him. Adjusting her legs so that she straddled him, he showed her by moving her hips in a ride what to do.

"Oh yes, oh yes. You're so deep." He watched her move, her breasts flushed with need. When he took her hands and cupped them, he nearly swallowed his tongue when she looked down at him while she pinched her nipples.

If he thought to slow things down, he realized this wasn't going to help. He sat up, took her offered nipple into his mouth, and slid his hand between them. Gathering her cream from her clit and stroking it, he moved to her rosette at her ass and rubbed her juices into the puckered entrance.

"I'm going to fuck you here," Austin told her as he circled the tight muscles. "I'm going to ram my cock deep into you and fuck you from behind. Would you like that? Want to feel my cock taking your ass?"

"Yes. Please…Austin, I'm coming." Her sheath rippled around his cock and nearly strangled him. When he felt his own release coming quickly now that she had, he rolled her back to the bed and slammed into her. He knew she'd be sore, but need ripped through him. With a final thrust, he came. His cock jettisoned deep and his fangs ached to mark. Licking the place where her shoulder met her neck, he bit.

Mine. Even as her blood filled his mouth, he could feel the bond forming. *Mine.* The bond that only mated couples felt. Nothing had prepared him for the overwhelming need to protect, to care for and to keep her. *Mine,* he thought over and over. Licking the wound again, his essences sealing the ragged opening, he nearly dropped on her, but rolled to his side again, pulling her lax body over his. His last thought before falling to sleep was that he'd forgotten about the person at the door.

~~~

CJ woke up tangled in the bed with Austin. Her body flushed with heat when she remembered what she'd begged him to do to her last night. Moving her hand to her neck where he'd bitten her, she expected it to come away bloody. But other than being slightly tender, it seemed fine. She moved to the edge of the bed and slid to the floor.

It only took her a moment to find her clothes and get dressed. She was starved, and was putting on her boots when she was suddenly pulled back into the bed. His mouth covered hers before she could utter a protest.

Heat filled her body as he tugged her down onto him. When he rolled her over onto her back, he grinned when her belly growled.

"We worked up an appetite, didn't we? I don't suppose I could persuade you to skip breakfast and let me make love to you all morning, could I?" Before she could answer, her belly growled again. "I'll take that as a no. Let me get dressed and I'll go with you. Besides, I want to see if I can smell who was at the door last night."

She flushed, remembering why he hadn't looked last night. She was suddenly glad his back was turned to her. She knew her face was flaming.

"I wonder if whoever it was thought I was alone and wanted to…I don't know, have dinner or something." She pulled on her boot and reached for the second one when she found herself back on the bed. "Austin?"

"I meant what I said last night, Charlie. No one can touch you. I'm a very jealous wolf and you're mine."

She remembered. But there was no reason for him to get all macho on her. She shoved him off her…or at least tried to. When that didn't work, she turned her head away. "Get off me. I'm quite capable of taking care of myself. I've been doing it for a long time." He didn't move for several seconds and she looked up at him. The look on his face confused her. He looked…well, he looked sad. Before she could ask him, he rolled off her and stood.

"Let's go. I'm starved too. Let me go out first. I want to see if I can scent anything."

She waited in the passenger seat while he climbed out the driver's, and watched him come around the side of the truck and sniff around. When he backed up several feet and shook his head, she nearly climbed out to see what happened. He looked like he got a whiff of something that didn't agree with him. He stopped her with a raised hand. Then he did the international sign for rolling down the window—a winding hand. She rolled her eyes as she reached over to turn the key to make the electric window go down.

"You know that crank windows are about faded out, right?" Then she asked, "What did you smell?"

She actually didn't feel as stupid as she thought she would asking him that. First of all, hello, man here, and secondly, after last night it was hard to deny that what he'd told her was anything but the truth.

"A male touched the door as recently as last night. A shifter...not wolf though. A cat, tiger." She started to ask if there were really weretigers, then snapped her mouth closed. Of course there were.

"I don't know any two-legged tigers." At least she didn't think so. "How will I tell when...am I a wolf now too?"

That was a weird thought. He'd bitten her and they'd had sex...boy had they had sex. He said he'd marked her, but hadn't he already done that? She decided she was going to make a list of questions to ask him so that she wouldn't feel so overwhelmed.

"No...not yet anyway. We'll talk about it. And you won't be able to tell. But I will. I have the scent now." He opened the door for her and she nearly got out. She turned back, put the window up, and took the keys. "Let's just pretend that nothing is out of the ordinary."

She snorted. "Okay. We'll just pretend that we didn't have this spectacular sex last night and that you didn't flip into a wolf and my—"

"Shift," he interrupted her. "I shifted. And was it really spectacular?"

She stopped to stare at him. *Not even going there*, she thought, and started toward the diner again. He grabbed her around the waist and pulled her to his body, his mouth covering hers in what could only be described as hot.

The world around them was fading away and all she could think of was the way his body was hard against hers when someone nudged her. She might have ignored them, but the second time she pulled away to yell, she was suddenly pulled into very tight arms.

"I'm so happy you worked out your differences. It's so nice to have another female around. Well there is Mom, but she isn't all that into shopping. Please tell me you like to shop. Oh my God, that would be just sinful if you don't. We'll have to go shopping for Christmas presents together. Won't that be so wonderful? And then—"

"Holly, take a breath. Christ, you could talk a deaf man to insanity." Austin kissed the woman on the cheek and then turned to stare at her when a low growl spilled from CJ's lips. She blushed.

"I'm sorry. I don't...I didn't even know I could...do you think you could step away from her? I have this urge to tear her eyes out and I don't much care for it."

The woman he called Holly stepped back and laughed. Austin pulled her back and grinned. "Charlie, this is my sister, Holly. Holly, meet my mate, Charlie Force."

The feeling of murder and mayhem dissipated. CJ mentally added another question to her growing list and walked into the diner with Holly on one side of her and Austin on the other.

"It's Webber. Not Force, just Webber. Glad to meet you, Miss Force."

CHAPTER THIRTEEN

Holly watched her brother with CJ. He probably didn't even know he was constantly touching her, but CJ did. She really seemed to be uncomfortable by it, Holly thought. Also, she kept correcting him when he called her Charlie. She told him several times she preferred to be called CJ.

"So, CJ, how long have you been a trucker?" Holly nearly burst out laughing when she asked. CJ had just moved to the other end of the booth only to be scooted back to Austin's side.

With a glare at Austin, CJ answered. "About eight years, give or take. Just after my mom died, so yeah, about eight years. She wanted me to become a lawyer and I decided I wanted away."

"So, you have any burning desire to go to school and realize her dream for you? Just for the record, my mom would have a cow if I suddenly became a trucker. But it sounds like fun." Holly smiled at the waiter as he set her food down. "But she loves me, so I'd be able to talk her into it."

Holly watched as CJ covered her hash browns in sausage gravy and then tore biscuits over the whole thing. When she reached for the hot sauce, Austin tried to take it from her, but CJ simply waited for him to put it down then threatened him with her fork before she answered.

"I had already gotten my law degree when she died. I had just started working with Phil when she—"

"You have a law degree, and you're driving a truck? What the hell for? This just goes to prove that I was right, and you will sell the rig and work on that instead of this ridiculous job driving around the country." Austin seemed satisfied with his pronouncement and started in on his breakfast. "As soon as this is over you'll sell the rig and move in with me at the pack house."

The fork rammed deep in the table and shimmied in the sunlight. Austin looked at it, then at CJ. Holly decided that she liked this girl more than she ever thought she would.

"Now that I have your attention," CJ said in a voice that made Holly want to obey. Alpha…CJ was an alpha female. "You will listen to me, because I don't plan to say this again. I had sex with you. Nothing more, nothing less. I am not your wife, I will not take your last name, and I most certainly will not sell my rig. When and if I decide I've had enough, I will set it aside. Not because you told me to, but because I want to. Where I live is not up to you. I'm a grown woman and I see to myself. Don't even start," CJ said when Austin opened his mouth. "This is not up for discussion."

CJ's cell phone rang and she picked it up, and without a word, she stood up and dug in her pocket as she answered the call. With a toss of her wrist, she threw forty dollars on the table and with a nod to Holly, CJ left.

Holly stared at her until she was out of sight. When Austin got up, Holly put her hand on his arm to stop him. "I wouldn't if I were you. Not if you plan to walk on your own in the future. She needs time to cool off, and you need time to learn that women are from the twenty-first century and not the dark ages." Holly slapped his arm. "What the hell is wrong with you? Are you stupid?"

"This is none of your business. This is between Charlie and me, and I would appreciate it if you minded your own business." He started to stand then sat back down, a look of total defeat on his face. "Fuck, I screwed that up. She just brings out the worst in me."

Holly laughed. "No, I'm pretty sure you do that all on your own. I've always thought you were a little overbearing, but this…Christ, Austin, you going to ground her if she doesn't obey you?"

"She doesn't understand. She's not even trying. I tell her to do something and she does the opposite just to piss me off. Damn it, Holly, she's human, and an independent one at that." Austin looked again at the doorway that CJ had gone through. "I don't know what to do about her."

Holly looked at her brother and almost felt sorry for him…almost. "Why does she not want you to call her Charlie? There must be a reason…maybe a bad memory that she has from…didn't you say her dad was that guy that shot Dallas? Maybe he called her that."

Austin looked at her and shook his head. "No, I call her that because that's her name, not to bring any bad memories to her. She should know I'd not do anything like that."

Holly picked up her water and tossed it in his face. When he stood up and reached out to grab her, she pulled her handgun and laid it on the table. He jerked his hand back as if she was a flame.

"Sit down." He sat. "Now, I'm going to ask you some questions and you'll answer them. You'll not yell and you most certainly will not snarl at me. Understand?"

"Where did you get that gun? You put that thing—" His mouth snapped shut when she picked it up.

"See how this works? Now, I noticed two things. One, and this is a biggie, you didn't know she has a law degree. Why? This brings me to number two. What's her birthday?"

115

Austin stared at her with his mouth open before answering. "What the hell does that have to do with her not listening to me?"

"So you don't know. And you never gave her the opportunity to listen, you fuck-tard, you made demands. I don't listen to demands either." She thought he mumbled she didn't listen to anything, but decided to let it go for now. "Her birthday is July tenth. I asked her in the ladies room." Holly had asked a few other things too, and most of those things she'd never tell her brother. "She hadn't spoken to her dad since the day her mom was buried. She lived with her grandma until she started driving a truck, and she is allergic to tape—anything sticky touches her skin and she blisters. What do you know?"

Austin growled low in his throat. "She was a virgin before last night and she's a pain in my ass."

"Yes, well, I'm betting you're no peach either." Holly saw CJ coming toward their table and looked at her brother. "You want her to hate you, then by all means continue treating her like Uncle Max did Aunt Susan. You remember what happened with that."

She'd had him killed. Paid a man twenty thousand dollars to murder her husband, then killed herself. Her note had said she was at peace for the first time in fifty years, approximately the same amount of time she'd been married to Uncle Max. She'd claimed she couldn't take his overbearing ways a minute longer.

"Charlie…CJ wouldn't hurt me. She's my mate." Holly didn't think he sounded so sure.

"Yes. But here's something to remember, I'm not your mate and I can hurt you." She stood up when CJ was five feet away. "Behave, Austin, and listen. You might be surprised by what you learn."

"I'm leaving," CJ said as she reached the table. She looked at Austin. "Why don't you go with your sister? That way I won't have to smother you in your sleep."

"I'm going. I told you I was and I am." Austin grabbed Holly in a tight hug and whispered in her ear, "I can't wait until you find your mate. I hope he makes your life a living hell."

Holly watched the big truck leave the lot and went to her car. Her brother would figure this out, she was sure. She was sliding into the seat when she thought about what he'd threatened her with. Smiling, she thought about her mate.

She knew who he was. She'd known for a very long time, but he didn't seem to. She wished things could be different, but she also knew that he wouldn't come to her. As she pulled into traffic, she wondered what her brother would say about that.

~~~

"Solomon called," CJ said as soon as they got on the highway again. "He wanted to know if we were going to make the deadline by Wednesday night or if we would need more time."

Austin looked over at her and frowned. "Does he think you're running behind? If so, how far does he think we are?"

"We're not behind. I'm right on...he mentioned my driving partner. I didn't tell him there was a passenger with me. He's watching. I'm not sure how much he knows yet, but he's watching me." She took out several sheets of paper and handed them to him as she continued. "Phil sent me that. It's from the Feds. Solomon is having this distributed for his stores across the United States. When I get this to the warehouse, it'll be re-boxed and then put on another truck going back this way."

Austin looked at the list. It detailed pages and pages of high end items—big screen televisions, computers, game systems, and even jewelry. He laid it on the console and looked at her.

"If they know what he's doing, then why are the Feds having you drive this to him? Why don't they simply arrest him and be done with it?" Austin thought he knew the moment he asked. He wasn't thrilled about what he thought was going on either.

Her answer confirmed it. "Because they want to see who the big cheese is. Phil seemed to think that Solomon is just the middleman, and that whoever we take this to is the one they want. They didn't even know the warehouse address until this."

Austin started to tell her that she'd have to tell them she wasn't doing it, but thought about what Holly had said. He tried to think of a tactful or even a nicer way to tell her she wasn't doing it, but the best he could do was tell her "no fucking way." He was sure that would go over well.

"I know what you're thinking and I'm taking this load, Austin. You should have gone with your sister if you think I'll not do this. I'm my own person, and you have no rights over me whatsoever."

It was on the tip of his tongue to tell her that she was his, but again, thought that it wouldn't be prudent. Instead, he tried reason. It could work.

"I'm telling you you're not." He winced when he realized that it hadn't been anywhere close to reason. "Let me reword that. It might have come out wrong."

"Oh no, you said it just like I thought you would." He could tell by her entire body she was pissed. "I've made arrangements for you to be picked up when we get to Amarillo, Texas. It's a good-sized town and they have a nice airport. I don't need the added stress of you for another three days."

She would leave him too. Austin wasn't sure if he was more hurt than pissed at her for making arrangements when he snapped his mouth closed. He'd done the same thing. Just as she'd done, he'd made arrangements to suit himself over her wants.

He looked out the window and thought. Christ, he didn't want to leave her. He didn't just want her…he needed her. Looking back at CJ, he tried again.

"I'll go home if after today you still want me to. I'm…it's been pointed out to me that I may have been a bit overbearing toward you."

"A bit? Austin, you've done nothing but order me around since the first time I saw you. I don't need it. No, I think for both of us we should just mark this as a bad experiment and move on with our lives." Austin could feel her hurt as she continued. "It's not worth the good sex. I won't have a man own me. My mother put up with it for nearly all her married life, and I won't."

He tried again. "I'm going to work on that. I swear. Just give me until Amarillo. If I haven't made some changes in my charming ways, I'll go willingly." He would leave her truck, but not her. He'd rent a car and follow her if need be, but he wouldn't leave her. "Please?"

Austin had never had to beg in his life, and never for the company of a woman. But he was beginning to realize she wasn't just any woman. She was his mate, his match.

"All right. But I'm not canceling the arrangements until we have to. I have to be honest with you, Austin. I can't take much more of this. You have to fucking back off. It was just sex. Nothing more."

Smiling to himself, he thought perhaps that she was saying that a little too much. She knew as well as he did that it wasn't just sex, and as soon as he could, he was going to prove it to her.

CHAPTER FOURTEEN

"They just passed over into Tulsa. She's about an hour from Oklahoma City. I figure they'll stop there for the night. I got another crew waiting for them there to see if she's got a tail or not."

Wayne Solomon looked over at his partner, Ruben Baker. He and Ruben had been working this same deal for over five years now, and it had been extremely profitable for them both. He looked around the room they were in and smiled.

The carpet alone cost more than most people made in a year. Italian made, it covered most of the knotty pine floor and was valued at just over ten million dollars. He grinned when he thought about how few people actually got to walk on this rug.

The antiques were the finest he could have. Most of the pieces were from an office he'd laid claim to several years ago. An antique dealer had kept a huge warehouse of beautiful things and when Wayne had tried to buy him out, he wouldn't sell. The man had very nicely left everything to Wayne when he'd died suddenly. An ice pick to the ear tended to do that.

The rest of his mausoleum was decorated the same way; beauty for only his eyes and those of the few people he had over. None of them were friends, not even Ruben, but they thought they were. Business was business and

Wayne had been very careful never to mix his pleasure with his business, though there were times when the two of them did spill over into one another.

"What do we know about the man traveling with her? Is he someone we need to be worried about?" They had been surprised when they'd seen the man with her yesterday, but not concerned. CJ Webber was a loner and too much like her father to have them worry about some man. The older Webber had been a business man too. Not a very good one, but a business man all the same.

"No. He still lives at home with his family. They have a nice bit of property next to where her father lived...the family he claimed was werewolves."

Wayne nodded. He remembered now. Webber had even said he'd shot one as it stole across his land. The police had gone out to the house of the man he'd said he'd shot and there was nothing. Wayne looked down at the file he'd had put together on CJ right after he'd gotten her name from a mutual contact.

"See that he doesn't become a problem. Make sure the claim of him being a wolf isn't true as well. I don't need any pack to show up when one of their brothers goes missing. As for Oklahoma City, make sure they get the tracer on her truck this time. Those idiots really bungled it last night."

The tracer the idiot...the dead idiot...had put on what he had assumed was the Webber girl's truck had instead been put on one going in the opposite direction from CJ. It took them nearly three hours to figure out what had happened, and by then it was too late to call off the kill of the driver. How was he to know that the man wasn't the right driver until it was too late? Totally and completely not his fault.

Wayne decided to call the girl that night, just to give her some encouraging words and maybe let her know that if she wasn't in on time, just a little off, he'd cut her some slack. Wayne loved the Wisconsin accent he'd perfected to talk to her. He had her eating out of his hands. Maybe when this run was over, he'd have to meet up with the pretty little trucker. Her picture, he was sure, didn't do her justice.

The load she was carrying for them was valued at just over fifty million. Preston Xpress had been shipping his jewelry in ordinary trucks for several weeks now. Diamonds and other gems were stashed in with the middle end televisions and the cheaper laptop computers. The floors were false, and only a few other than store managers where the merchandise was going had any idea what they were receiving. The trucks, unloaded by the staff, would be stolen into late at night so that the manager could get in and get the things that had been hidden. Wayne had only found out about it several days ago...in fact, on the same day he'd called little Miss Webber.

Ruben's phone went off. From the ring tone, Wayne knew it was Ruben's wife. The man was a simpering fool when it came to his mate. There were days, like today as a matter of fact, that he wished Ruben would just shoot her, then himself. It mattered little to Wayne that Ruben's wife was his own sister...she was a whiny bitch. By the time Ruben had ended the call, Wayne wanted to hit someone. Instead, he sent Ruben on any errand.

"Find out what you can about this supposed wolf. I want to know if he is a loner or is he a member of a pack. If he is I want to know how big it is and if he will be missed."

"You want to get him away from the girl? Are you thinking he'll be an issue?" Ruben took out his phone and began clicking away at the keys. "I can have someone...that new guy, what was his name? Isaac Dorsey can hunt them down. I'm betting he can—"

"No. No more outsiders. I want you to do this. This load can make us very rich, and I would like to be able to spend it without having to look over my shoulder all the time." Wayne had plans to not look over his shoulder and see Ruben and his family there already. "Go to Oklahoma City and see what you can find out. Report back to me. I'm going to go to Columbus and see what I can find there."

Wayne waited until Ruben left for the airstrip and then sat behind his desk. Pulling out the list from under his blotter, he checked off two of his "to do" things. Number three, check on Webber girl, done. Number twelve, kill Ruben—here he put half a check mark. Smiling, he knew that it would only be a matter of hours before that little item was checked as well. The other two things he checked were getting rid of the car he'd stolen two weeks ago and selling off the few pieces of antiques that he no longer found enjoyable.

He picked up his disposable phone and called CJ. She answered on the second ring. That made him smile. He could not abide rudeness...not of any kind.

~~~

Austin had started to doze off again when the dash exploded with static. He looked over at CJ as she played around on a radio-looking device that sat above her stereo. So far as he could see, she didn't listen to music, so he couldn't figure out what station she'd be trying to tune into this far into the trip. Then when voices came through the line, he realized it was a CB.

If anyone would have asked Austin, he would have said that CBs were a thing of the past. He thought that with cell phones and satellite, no one would have any use for them in this day and age. He started to ask her about it when a very clear, very male voice sounded out of the thing.

"That you QT-Pie? Damn girl, you said you's done. How the heck are you?"

Austin's breath caught when CJ smiled. He didn't think he'd ever seen anything more beautiful.

"Yeah, Jungle Jock, it's me. You know how it is, can't stay still for more than ten seconds without my legs getting all jumpy."

Austin sat back to listen.

"You knows it. I been doing this so long my butt's got big old calluses on it. Makes my bottom look like a horse's south end." They both laughed at the unseen man. "Hear it told you done purchased that farm. Whatcha doin' that for? You gonna make your dream happen?"

CJ glanced over at Austin before she answered. "Umm, yeah. Got a deal too good to pass up. Construction starts in the thaw. Should be up and running by next spring if all goes well."

"Your momma'd be prouder than a peacock. You got a name picked out? Should be something fitting. I think it should be—"

"Hey Jungle, what do you know of the Mounties coming through Tex-ass? I got me a load I have to get on time." Austin raised a brow at her as she continued. "I have less than two days to get to the City of Angels."

"Ah hell, girly, ain't seen nothing of them for several hours. I was thinking there was a donut convention going on and they all got themselves an invite. Hope so, 'cause me and the boys we are making up for lost time." Austin glanced over at the speedometer and winced. Eighty. If she got pulled over, they'd all be sunk. He felt the truck begin to slow and looked again at the dash. Seventy now.

After ten more minutes or so of bantering back and forth, Austin saw her turn the thing down. He could see signs for Oklahoma City and wondered how much further she was planning to go that day. Frankly, his own ass was getting to be a tad sore and he wanted to stretch.

They'd been in the truck since six that morning. They had stopped once around noon to get gas and to go to the bathroom. She'd filled up while he went inside, and when she'd gone in to go to the bathroom, he'd taken the opportunity to call Phil, then Dallas.

Phil hadn't answered so he left a message telling him where they were and they were both fine, then he'd called his brother.

"Hey, I found out what the trust is for." Dallas launched right into it as soon as he answered. "She bought about four thousand acres just outside of Columbus. From the county records, she's applied for a building permit to build a set of apartments. The city is all for it, of course. She got a tax abatement for ten years, and then she's guaranteed to hire twenty people by the end of the first year."

"It's an apartment? Are you sure?" Austin knew it was something more than that. And Dallas confirmed it.

"That's what they are calling it now. One of the pack works for the county engineer's office and he said that it's being called that to hide what it really is. Austin, it's going to be the Rebecca Jane House. It's a place for battered and abused women. It'll even have health care and some learning facilities when it's complete." Austin lay back on the bed as his brother continued. "There's something else. Your mate? She's rich. Not just rich, but 'oh my fucking God' rich. Not counting the three properties that she'll sign off on in January, she's worth well over ten million. Once she signs off on that, she'll be a cool twenty. I've already got an appointment with Phil to make him the pack's financial guru."

Austin heard the door open and took a deep breath through his mouth. CJ; her scent made his cock harden. When she walked through the doorway with two bags of what smelled like burgers and fries, Austin told his brother he'd call him later.

After they ate, CJ got back at the wheel and Austin sat in the passenger side to think. That had been nearly four hours ago. They'd only said a handful of words since. But looking at her now, Austin could see the fatigue written all over her face.

"How much longer are you going today? You look like you can barely hold your head up." She glanced over at him, but didn't say anything. "CJ, why don't we pull over and rest? You could nap for an hour of two and probably feel a lot better."

"I can't. If I can make it to Amarillo tonight, you'll be on a plane home by midnight. Phil set it up for you." They passed the sign welcoming them to Sayre, Oklahoma just as she finished. "There's an airport, Rick Husband Amarillo International Airport, that's just a few miles from the Love's I'm going to be staying at to—"

"No. Don't send me back. I've been...I can't leave you, CJ. Not when you're this close to getting this finished. What if something happens?" He took a deep breath before he spoke again. "Even if you don't let me ride with you, I'll rent a car and follow you."

He could see tears forming in her eyes. He was honest with her. She could drop him off at the airport, but she couldn't make him leave. And he wouldn't. Not now...not ever. He saw her nod, and he felt like she'd given him permission to take a deep breath. Since that morning when she'd told him she couldn't do this any longer, he'd been afraid...terrified really...that she'd turn him away.

Austin watched her as they drove on. Another three hours, she told him, and she'd pull into the Love's to rest. Then another ten hours on Tuesday, and she'd be only about six hours or less to Los Angeles. Before he could comment, her cell phone rang. She looked over at him before she reached above her head and turned the phone on.

"Hello, Miss Webber. You must be getting close to Oklahoma City, don't you know. Some of the other drivers are going to help you bring the load in. Their names are—"

"I'm already past Oklahoma City. I didn't stop there." When CJ looked over at him, Austin could see the slight anger in her eyes. Before she could continue, Solomon did.

"I see. So where exactly are you and your rider, Miss Webber?" The coldness in his voice was tangible, even through the phone. "I mean, are you even bringing me my load?"

She didn't answer, though Austin could tell that she wanted to. But she did something that surprised him. She reached above her head where the cell was clipped and put her finger over it.

"No one has ever questioned my honesty before, and neither will you." She cut Solomon off in mid sputter and pushed the end button.

When the large rig started making its way to the side of the road, Austin held his breath. She was watching what she was doing, but that didn't make it any less scary when horns blared and tires screamed.

"I need to...I'm pissed and I can't drive." He simply nodded, too afraid to say anything to distract her. When she turned off the key, he looked at her.

She was shaking. He'd never seen her this...well, emotional, he thought. When he started to reach for her shoulder, she turned and started toward him. When her hand was on the handle to get out of the door, she slipped and fell against him.

Need, which had been coiled up inside him since that morning, leapt out at her, and he groaned at the contact. Before he could think whether or not it was a smart move, he cupped the back of her neck and brought her mouth to his.

Her mouth opened under his assault. Then he wasn't sure who was taking whom. Hands grabbed at his shoulders as she settled herself over his lap. His cock lengthened beneath her and he surged up into her heat.

"CJ, I want you. Now. I want…no, I need…to bury my cock deep into you." She rocked into him as her answer. "Christ."

He shifted her legs so that they were on either side of his hips. Cupping her ass, he brought her to his cock as she rocked on her knees onto him. Austin felt his beast swirl under his skin, the need to mate with her overwhelming.

Her hands pulled and tugged at his shirt as he devoured her mouth. He could smell her need and it smelled like manna to him. Lifting her shirt, he took her nipple into his mouth along with her lacy bra and sucked hard. Her body bowed back, a moan spilling from her lips.

He tore at her pants, pulling them down over her ass and cupping the globes of hot flesh that he found himself wanting to sink his teeth into. Lifting her off his lap, she whimpered. Pushing her back against the console, Austin tore at his own snap and zipper and freed his cock.

"Take them off. Take them off before I shred them from you." His voice was deep with need, the beast making him growl more than speak. But she seemed to understand and was soon standing before him in only her shirt he'd pulled up over her breasts and her ravaged bra.

Jerking her forward, he impaled her over him, bringing her down hard on his cock even as he surged up into her. Austin felt her channel ripple and tighten around him. Her body primed for him, she came screaming his name as she dug her nails deep into his shoulder.

He wanted to fuck her. He wanted to roll her to her back and pound into her pussy until he spilled his seed deep. But there was no room, the seat and the small cab making it impossible for them to do more than what they were doing. Austin braced his feet on the floor, and holding her hips to him, surged up again and again.

When he felt her body tightening again, he reached between them and thumbed her clit. He could feel her juices as they creamed on his balls.

"Come," he demanded. "Come again. Now, CJ, come now."

Her body, already tight, detonated. She screamed out her release in a long shudder. He was so mesmerized by her face, the way her sheath milked and pulled at his cock, that when his own climax hit him, he roared, his wolf snarled for release, and he couldn't stop him.

The wolf bit her. Austin felt the warm rush of blood as it slid down his throat and he drank greedily from her. CJ whimpered as she fell limply over him. With a final swipe of his tongue, he sealed the wounds, a scar already forming there of his long snout teeth marks. She was his.

The mark on her neck would remain, and unlike the one he'd given her earlier, this one would be visible to everyone. This was a mark of possession, the one the wolf, his wolf, had given her. Austin could no more leave her now than cut off his own leg. She was his as surely as if they had been united by a divine entity. Austin shifted her in his lap and looked down at her face.

Her eyes were closed, but he knew she wasn't asleep. He gently ran his finger down her cheek and watched as her eyes fluttered open. She flushed, her skin heated until it was a dusky rose, and she started to pull away.

"Don't," he said as he held her to his body. "Not yet. I know we'll have to move soon, but not yet."

"I'm sorry. You must think…I have no idea what you think of me for this." She flushed darker as she turned her head into his neck.

Austin pulled her chin up to see into her eyes. "I think you're a very passionate woman who used sex instead of violence to relieve the pressure. And anytime you need to let off any more steam, please don't hesitate to use me."

She laughed as he had hoped she would.

CHAPTER FIFTEEN

She started driving the rest of the way to the truck stop. Love's, a national chain, was only another one hundred and fifty miles from where she'd pulled over. Her body, lax and sated, seemed to hum now. She glanced over at Austin, who was looking at her as she drove.

"What?" She shifted in her seat, suddenly uncomfortable with what she'd done to him. "You could have said 'no,' you know."

"Not that I wanted to, but I doubt you would have listened. I find myself wondering what else is behind that cool façade." He reached over and ran his fingers down her arm resting on the shifter. "You are the most responsive woman I know. I want to take you to the sleeper, rip your clothes from your delicious body, and lick you until you come. I want to taste your pussy again, feast on it until I get enough."

CJ shifted again on her seat, this time to try and relieve some of the ache her body had because of what he was telling her. Before she could respond, her phone rang again. She looked up to see that it was unknown again. With a groan, she opened the connection with a quick "hello."

"My dear, I must apologize," Solomon said in greeting. "I can't tell you how badly I feel, don't you know. I've just been...well, I've been so stressed about this weather and this load along with two others. I cannot tell you enough how sorry I am. You have my deepest and most profound apologies."

"I'm not a thief. I told you I'd be there on Wednesday night and I will be. I'm a woman of my word." CJ glanced over at Austin, who tapped her on the shoulder.

He leaned so close to her that she could feel his heat. Even as he whispered in her ear, she could hardly concentrate on the words as her body reacted to his. Christ, she was a walking nymphomaniac and she only wanted this man. When what he said registered after he pulled back, she nodded. She realized she missed whatever Solomon was saying.

"...to me I can have someone help you the rest of the way in. I feel just horrible that you've put yourself and your rider in danger by driving nearly non-stop."

"I'm fine. We're both fine." She looked over at Austin and he nodded before she continued. "If we get in late to the warehouse, who will meet us there? I mean, I don't know you from Adam, so I'd like to know a name or two."

She heard papers move around much like the sound that Phil made when he was stalling. She smiled when she realized she'd put this man off balance. When he started speaking again, she knew that he'd gotten ahold of himself now, but he'd be more careful in the future with her.

"I'll be there, of course. Also a few other men to unload. I'll give you my personal number to call me when you are close. That way I can meet you there and tell you in person what a wonderful job you've done for me."

"That won't be necessary. I just want to be able to sleep for a few hours before I head back. You just be there and I'll call you when I'm an hour out."

He assured her he would be, and then after a few more apologies and another thank you, they disconnected. CJ drove for another twenty minutes before she spoke again. When she did, Austin burst out laughing.

"I don't see why you think that's a funny question. I think it's important to know if the man is a big dog or not."

"Its alpha, love, not big dog. I'm a wolf, not a pup." She glanced over at him and felt her body flush with need. Nope, Austin wasn't a pup.

"I don't even know what that means other than what I've read in smut books. The alpha male runs the pack and everyone obeys his every whim. If you think I'm going to be doing that, then you're nuttier than a fruit cake."

He laughed again. "No, I'm beyond thinking you'll listen to me. As for my every whim...that does have its merits, but also not true. I guide my pack."

She snorted. "Sure you do. Like you tried to guide me, no doubt. I'm not saying that I'm going to go along with whatever you say, but I do have some questions."

He moved his leg up in the seat and looked at her. She couldn't help but think about the way he'd taken her in that very seat a while ago and she shifted again. Christ, if this kept up she was going to be pregnant for sure.

"Babies. Holy shit, I forgot to take my pill yesterday and today. I knew it was a mistake to have you...you know, come in me. Now...will I have puppies or babies?"

"Whelp. And no, children are born as human, and if you were primed to get pregnant with me, the birth control pill wouldn't work. As my mate, it is your duty to...don't get all pissy, let me finish." She opened her mouth to snarl at him about the duty word and closed it again when he held up his hand. "By duty, I mean to continue the line of our race. The sperm of a wolf is stronger than that of any man made deterrent. It's like that because of my race, not because I deem it so."

She stared out the window, wondering how to ask this next question. "I don't know a great deal about sex. I wondered...is it always so, you know, passionate?"

That seemed a tame word for what they had done. When she was with him, it seemed like she was another person, one that was so uninhibited that she didn't know herself. She wondered if it would be like that with any other man, and decided that she'd never ask him that even if she wanted to aggravate him. He just seemed to be really possessive around her.

"Passionate. I would say what we've been doing borders on the near violent. But no, it's not like that between humans…at least not from what I've experienced." She glanced over at him when he didn't finish.

"But you've had sex with other…humans, right? I mean, do you bite them? Do you…you know, come like that?" She hated that even after what they had shared, what she'd done to him, that she could be embarrassed about asking him questions.

"I've bitten women to hold them still, but not like I have you. The mark I made on you tonight is my brand. You belong to me. My mate." He touched her arm again. "Do you feel it when I touch you? Feel the way the mark burns? It's to remind you that you belong to me. When I'm near you, when I touch you, it will let you know that you belong to me."

That didn't bother her as much as it had even yesterday, him telling her that she belonged to him; nor did the fact that his brand marred her skin. She shivered again when she thought of his teeth sinking into her skin, the way it had felt to have him bite her so hard. She glanced over at him when he growled.

"I can smell your arousal. It's like your body is calling to mine. If you don't want to pull over again and let me take you to the sleeper, I suggest you find a less intense subject." She knew he adjusted his cock in his pants and she wished it was that easy for her. "Tell me about this project you and Phil have set up."

She didn't even wonder how he knew. She figured that he had someone watching over her, probably Dallas. She didn't want to tell him about the shelter, but she figured he more than likely knew about as much as she did but was trying to distract her. She started telling him about the property first.

"It's right outside of town. I saw it a while back, but the property had been in foreclosure for so long I'd just about given up on it. It's just over five thousand acres of prime land that has a pond and several out buildings on it. It had been used as a retreat for a religious organization several years ago, but they couldn't keep the taxes up…or so the preacher said. He was skimming off the top almost all the way to the bottom."

"That's a big piece of property. What is it you're going to do with it…besides the shelter, I mean?"

She had expected him to tell her she was stupid, but when he seemed genuinely interested, she smiled. "I have several other things in the works as well. I figured that I'd build on the other end, far enough away so that I could hide when I wanted to. There's a house there, big and full of bedrooms, that would be easy to lose myself in. An apple and peach orchard are on one side, and there is a plum and pear orchard on the other. There was once a garden. I think that at one time there was a place where the owner sold their crops to the town, though no one seems to be sure." She could almost see it as she told him. "The house and the surrounding fifty acres aren't a part of the five thousand, but it does bump up against it. I've had it for several years. I've been having it worked on, sort of bringing some of it up to code while I tried to think what I wanted to do with it."

Phil knew she'd bought it, probably even knew she'd been working on it. But neither of them had mentioned it over the years. She had planned to move into it for a few months as soon as this run was over and just hide.

"Will you show it to me? When we get back, will you show me what you've done?"

She waited for him to say so he could tell her what she'd done wrong, but he didn't, so she agreed. "It's not far from your land. It's about ten miles south of your land and the property my father lived in. The house sits in the middle of the land, then the land for the shelter is just on the other side of it."

He laughed. "You mean the Sanders place? The pack and I have been running that land since we moved here several years ago. I had...the house, it's nearly as big as an apartment building. How many rooms does it have?"

"Ten bedrooms and five baths...well, now it does. It had two bathrooms on the upper level and one on the lower. I've had more put in. So, you know where it is?"

"Yes, it's lovely. The fruit trees, you've had them taken care of. The last full moon of the fall, my mom took a basket with her, and after our run she filled it with some of the fruit. It was going to waste. I hope you don't mind."

She shook her head. "No. Maybe someday she can make me a pie or something for them. Phil suggested that I learn to make jam. Screw that, I want to sink my teeth into an apple right now."

The truck stop was just ahead and she started making her way to it. Exhaustion and hunger made her want to hurry, but the traffic made her cautious. She moved to the turn lane and pulled in. A shower was first on her list of things to do, then a big dinner. In less than twenty-four hours, she'd be in California and this load finished.

~~~

Wayne was sitting in the destruction of his living room when his phone rang. He picked up the receiver to the house phone without bothering to look at the caller ID. He was so pissed about what that stupid cunt had done to him that he could barely see straight.

"Yes, what it is? This isn't a good time. You'll have to call me back." He nearly hung up when the person stopped him.

"It's Elliot Osborn with the Michigan State police, Mr. Solomon. We've...I've been trying to contact you concerning your partner and his family. There's been...there's been an accident."

Wayne had forgotten about the plane. Damn it all to hell and back. The girl had made him forget that he was supposed to be watching the news when the report of the plane going down came in so he could see it all unfold. Now he had to listen to this creep and pretend he wasn't thrilled beyond words about Ruben being dead.

"Ruben Baker? He's not here. I think he's on his way...a vacation, I think he said. He and his family are going on a trip to the Poconos or something. You'll have to call him at his home later." It wasn't hard for Wayne to fake the anger in his voice. He was livid right now.

"Mr. Solomon, I'm afraid you're misunderstanding me. Your partner and his family, they've been killed. The plane they were in went down over the Canadian border about eight hours ago. Best we can tell, everyone on the little plane died on impact. I'm so sorry."

Damn right they went down...and they had already been dead. The exhaust being filtered into the cabin had killed them all, including the pilot, well before they hit the ground. Wayne had seen an episode on television on how that had been done, and had gone out to the little plane and done it himself. His boss thought it was too funny.

Arthur Sims had been his boss and sometimes friend for nearly all his life. Wayne had felt, especially recently, that he'd outgrown the older man and thought it might be time to move on. He wanted the man to leave him the business, but he wanted it now instead of later. The person on his phone brought him back to the conversation.

"Ruben had three children, like my own kids to me...please tell me that they are all right." Wayne knew they weren't. He'd insisted that Ruben take them with him, to make it a sort of getaway for them as well.

"Three? I think…yes, there were only two children on board. I don't think…I don't believe they had three children. Let me check on that—"

"I'm sorry, grief you know. I'm just not thinking right." Wayne mentally kicked himself. He didn't have a clue how many kids Ruben and his sister had, he was just glad that they'd all been on the plane.

Officer Osborn went on for several more minutes. Something about making arrangements, seeing to the family's needs. Wayne listened to about a third of it, probably less than that if he was honest. After the officer started making noises about coming out to the house, just to make sure Mr. Solomon understood what had happened to his friend and colleague, Wayne decided he'd had enough. After assuring him that he was fine, Wayne simply put the phone back on the cradle.

He looked around the room he'd destroyed when the cunt had hung up on him. If it wasn't for his load she hauled, he'd hunt her down and make her pay for each and every broken item in the room. But for now, he had to focus.

She had his merchandise and she wasn't cooperating with him. This thing with her bringing in a second person had bothered Ruben, but not him or Arthur. It gave her something else to focus on except for the load. Yes, having the man along would also serve to make her more congenial, someone to keep her in line. But that hadn't worked out either. He knew then that her rider wasn't anything more than a weak pup. No real wolf would let her get by with the way she'd talked to him.

His phone ringing startled him. Lifting the receiver after seeing who it was made Wayne straighten in his chair and fix his mussed hair. He knew that Arthur couldn't see him, but it was a point of his to be well groomed at all times.

"Yes, sir. How may I help you?"

"I suppose you've heard about this thing with Baker. Terrible mess that was. I wish you'd of made me aware of just how you were going to knock him off. Might have taken a little trip with them this time, and then where would you be?"

Wayne felt his heart rate speed up. The man was entirely too perceptive. "Yes, sir. That would…. Why would you think I'd do something like that?"

"Because you're a greedy bastard and would murder your own mother—well, in this case your own sister—to get more of the cut. Well, did you?"

Wayne didn't like this. They were on a regular phone and there could be others listening, or someone could be in Arthur's house right now listening in, just waiting for him to mess up. Instead of answering, he changed the subject.

"The Webber girl is almost to Amarillo. She should be in Cally just like she said. She's been a bit…well, she was a bit smart with me today when I last spoke to her." Wayne looked around the room. "She needs to be made aware of who is paying her."

"Got smart with you, did she? Good for her. And on time too. Maybe I should have her working for me instead of an idiot like you. And don't think I didn't notice that you changed the subject." The laugh that came across the line to Wayne made him want to find him and shoot his face off. "I want to meet her. You let me know when she comes in. I will be there too. Now that you've taken care of whatever you perceived your problem with Baker was, I might need to take on someone else to help with making me money."

Wayne was still sputtering when Arthur hung up on him. Wayne took several deep breaths to try and calm his anger, but sitting in one of his favorite rooms with his things broken didn't help. He lifted the glass of bourbon near his hand and threw it at the large screen television that had until then missed any of the carnage.

Standing and shifting at nearly the same moment, Wayne launched himself through the glass door and took off for the backyard and the woods beyond. He needed relief, relief so profound he could barely see through the red haze and the pounding headache.

The first thing he scented was human. Sliding up behind it on his belly, Wayne attacked the gardener and ripped his throat out. But it wasn't enough. He needed to hurt, destroy, and to kill. Raising his snout to the air, he found several more humans. Feeling his body surge with the need to hurt, he followed their scents and killed them all.

By the time he returned to the house, his body, human now, was covered in blood. He could feel the hot, sweet essences of them pounding in his veins and his body felt stronger for it. He was coming through the broken glass when he saw his housekeeper. A pretty little thing, he decided, and felt his cock harden with need. She looked up from picking up some broken glass and started to back away.

"If you run, I will kill you. If you suck me off, then you may not get fucked. Up to you." He stroked his cock, the sticky blood making the move smooth. "Down on your knees, and you'd better not miss a drop."

She moved to her knees, her body trembling with need, he thought. Well, she'd get more than she bargained for if she wanted him inside of her. He wasted no time and yanked her head back by grabbing a handful of her hair. After snarling for her to open, he rammed his cock into her mouth and fucked her to the back of her throat.

Her screams only gave him more of what he needed, and after only a few seconds, he spilled his seed down her mouth. As soon as he finished, he dropped her to the floor and walked over her.

"Clean this mess up," he told her as he strode to the door. "And if you tell one person, even your mother, I will hunt her down and do what I should have done to you—fucked you until I ripped you apart. Do you understand me?"

When she nodded, tears in her eyes, he left the room and headed for his bedroom and a shower. He felt measurably better and smiled when he thought of the cunt trucker. She was going to pay when he saw her, and so was Arthur Sims.

CHAPTER SIXTEEN

Austin watched CJ move toward the showers with her bag over her shoulder. He moved to the men's room and quickly scrubbed his body and got dressed. Austin had plans. As he made his way to the dining room he asked to speak to the manager.

"I need a dinner for two to go. My wife has been driving all day and, well, I'd like to do something special for her." Austin hoped CJ hadn't heard him refer to her as his wife again. Even as tired as she was, she'd probably hurt him. "She's…well, I've made her mad and I want to make it up to her."

Austin wasn't sure why he admitted to the man that he'd pissed her off. He figured that he'd do whatever it took for him to get her to let him stay with her. The man looked to be about Austin's age and he also wore a wedding band.

"What did you do? The reason I'm asking is to see if whatever you're doing might work for me. I sort of forgot our anniversary yesterday. Not the wedding one…I remember that one, but the first date one. How is a man supposed to remember all the stuff they do?"

Austin didn't know. He decided to get himself a notebook and start writing things in it. First and foremost, he was going to write the date he'd met her and the night he'd taken her virginity.

"I'm going to take her a nice dinner to the rig, feed her, then when she's full, I'm going to give her a full body massage. When she's finally asleep, I'm going to watch her sleep and thank my lucky stars she's allowed me into her life." Austin realized that he was lucky. She was his world and he hadn't shown her that. He decided if this guy wouldn't help him, he'd go to the fast food joint on the other end and get them burgers and fries to keep her happy.

"Yeah, okay. Women like that sappy stuff. I'll fix it for you. But you'll let me know how it works out. I need to do something. I haven't had sex in over two weeks. I'm hurting, if you know what I mean."

Austin didn't comment. This guy would be lucky if his wife didn't cut his dick off in his sleep. Sappy stuff? Austin looked over at the bathroom again and didn't see CJ. He had the keys so he knew she couldn't get by him. Twenty minutes later, the manager and CJ found him at the same time.

"Oh good," CJ told him as the manager handed him the bag. "You got you something to go. I'm not hungry, so I think I'll go back and sleep. I didn't realize how tired I was until I got all warm from the shower." Nodding, Austin followed her out.

She was dressed in what he could only describe as a handkerchief. Her legs, long and incredibly well toned, stretched for a good mile. The tight blue jean skirt seemed to have a life of its own the way it moved and swayed with each of her steps. The shoes, small flip-flops, showed off her tiny feet and the pale pink polish that topped each toe. But it was her shirt that had him wanting to shove his fist into his mouth and whimper like a small animal.

Her back was completely bare, with only a small knot of material at the base of her spine to hold the shirt together. When he'd seen her coming toward him, he felt his entire body get hard and his cock seep with need. Her breasts, unfettered by a bra, bounced with her movements, and even though he knew she wasn't aware of it, every man, and even most women, noticed her nipples.

It was all Austin could do not to throw her over the breakfast bar and take her from behind, to mark her again as his, and to fill her body with his seed. Moving closer behind her, just to protect her, he told himself, he felt her heat, smelled the soft scent of her shampoo and the scent of his wolf all over her. A small growl escaped his mouth before he could stop it. When she stopped and looked over her shoulder at him, he nearly dropped to his knees and begged her to let him taste her.

"Are you all right?" she asked him softly. "I don't think I've ever heard you growl except when you're pissed or horny. Which are you now?"

Austin moved up behind her and rocked his cock into her ass. "Right now I'm pissed because I'm not deep inside of you. Go before we're arrested."

"Arrested? What for? Walking to the rig? Get real." She was out the door before he pulled her body to his from behind. "Austin?"

"Arrested for fucking you in front of everyone that walks by us." He snarled close to her ear. "Go, or I swear all my good intentions are going to be for naught. I'm hard enough right now to bend you over the closest car and take you."

She stared for all of five seconds before her scent hit him. Another growl sent her moving to the rig and he followed her, taking deep breaths. She was going to kill him. He knew it as surely as he was living. Trying to keep his mind on the fact that she was his forever and he didn't need to fuck her right away only worked so long as he wasn't watching her hips and ass sway in a way that beckoned him to come after her. He was in so much trouble.

She was standing next to the driver's door when he finally made it to the rig. He had better control over himself, but not much. She looked fuckable, and he wanted to oblige her in so many ways. Unlocking the door and watching her climb into the truck broke him, and he took the stairs just behind her and flattened her on the seat before she could get in.

"I need you. Now." He rocked into her, the bag of food in his hand forgotten. "Go to the bed and get on your hands and knees. This is going to be fast and hard."

She didn't say a word, but hurried to do what he wanted. He could smell her now. Her scent was driving him on. When she disappeared into the sleeper, he followed, dropping the food on the other seat and unsnapping his jeans as he went.

She was on the bed as he'd directed. She hadn't removed her clothes, for which he was glad and angry. He wanted to strip them off and he wanted them gone. As soon as he was behind her, he lifted the tiny skirt up off her ass and did whimper then.

A thong. Not a pretty little colored either, but a bright fire engine red. Austin wrapped both his hands in the tiny ribbons on either side and tore them from her. Her moan was enough to let him know that she was ready. Reaching between her legs with his fingers, he found her wet, dripping wet, and hot.

"Fuck, CJ. You're going to hate me for this." He rammed his cock deep. His hands held her steady as he took her, pounding into her heat and wet channel like a mad man. When her hand cupped his balls, he looked down at her and saw his cock soaked with her juices and her hand fondling him. It sent him over the edge and he roared out his release. Even as he reached around her and pinched her clit, he could feel her tighten around him, and each surge into her got tighter and tighter. When she exploded, her climax screaming from her throat, Austin felt another smaller but no less powerful climax grab him. He dropped over her and took her to the bed.

He couldn't move. His entire body felt as though he'd been put through a ringer and had come out the other side broken yet sated. He rolled to his back, his cock still semi-hard deep in her, and brought her with him. When he thought he could speak and make sense, he chuckled.

"I had meant to make this enjoyable for you. I wanted to make love with you, not take you like a rutting animal." When she turned and looked at him, his breath caught. "Christ, you're beautiful."

"Thank you. And what makes you think I didn't enjoy this? I came very hard when you did." She moved off him as she continued. "But I think I would like to see more than just a small glimpse of you. But not tonight...I'm exhausted."

She started to stand and he stopped her. He wanted her again, but not with the urgency he'd had earlier. Austin stood up, pulled her into his arms, and she wrapped her arms around his waist.

"I have dinner for us. Then I want to strip you down and massage you." Her hum of approval made his cock twitch. "Then while you sleep, I'm going to hold you the rest of the night."

He pulled her away from him long enough to take her shirt off. "Don't wear this in public again, please. It's enough to cause a riot. Besides, it makes me pissy when other men look at you."

Her giggle made him smile. He wanted to hear it again and again. As he was turning her around so that her back was to him, he stilled.

He was in love with her. When she turned and looked at him, her face full of concern, he turned her back around until he could think and began to unbutton her skirt. His mind was about half on his task and nearly missed what she was saying.

"I love this shirt, thanks. It's going to be so hot tonight here. I love the weather, but I wouldn't want to live here. I love the seasons in Ohio. By the time we get to California, it's going to be too hot to wear much more than this."

The skirt slid to the floor and he brought his hands to her waist as he buried his face in her shoulder. She smelled like his wolf. He reached for one of his shirts and handed it to her. Taking a small nip of her wrist when she took it, he told her to sit down.

"I got us some food. It's probably cold by now." He reached to the seat and brought the large bag to the bed. "I wanted this to be so romantic for you. I don't even know what that guy fixed us."

The meal turned out to be roast beef sandwiches and large containers of potato salad. He burst out laughing when he realized how much more trouble the guy was in than he thought if this was a romantic dinner. He told CJ about their conversation.

"Maybe the guy doesn't know how to romance a woman," CJ said as she took a huge bite of the sandwich. "There was this girl in college. She wanted her boyfriend to romance her. He brought some of his magazines over and wanted her to do what the women were doing to the guys on the pages."

Austin waited for her to finish and when she didn't, he prompted her. "You mean like Penthouse and Playboy? Tell me that didn't work. And please tell me that you didn't watch."

She looked at him with so much shock that he burst out laughing. "No, thank you very much, I did not watch. And yes, it did work. She married the guy as soon as the semester was over. I think they have like seven kids or something."

He watched her finish her food as her eyes got heavier and heavier. Taking the remnants of their dinner off the bed, he pulled her down to the mattress. Starting at her feet, he began to massage her toes and worked his way up her calves. She moaned several times but said nothing. When he realized she was asleep, he pulled the cover up over her and turned out the lights. He stepped outside the rig and called Phil.

"I'm in love with her," he told the vamp when he answered. "Falling over my lower lip, heart pounding, toe curling in love with her." The fucking bastard laughed. "I'm serious. What the hell am I supposed to do now?"

"Hope the hell she loves you back. Because I got news for you, she's the real deal. But you hurt her and I'll hunt you for the rest of your days and then drain you." Austin believed him. "Where are you right now?"

"Amarillo, Texas. Tomorrow she said we'd get to Kingman, Arizona. Then from there we're only about five hours from the warehouse. She said I can stay, if you are wondering."

She hadn't, but she hadn't mentioned him going back either. Austin started to explain that to the man, but he spoke first.

"So, from where you'll be tomorrow, you'll be about…let me see…."

Austin closed his eyes. He wanted to go back in and cuddle up with his mate, not try and figure out the vampire who knew her better and was talking in riddles. Austin looked at the empty lots surrounding them and wondered if he could shift and go for a quick run when Phil came back.

"You're going to be just a bit over two hours from Vegas. You want me to book you a room and a wedding chapel?" Austin sat down hard as Phil continued. "I can have a limo pick you up if you know where you're going to stay, take you to the chapel, and then bring you back to the rig sometime after noon. You'll still make the deadline and you'll be married too."

Married. He looked over his shoulder at the door that his mate was sleeping behind. He rubbed his hand over his heart and realized he wanted to do this more than he wanted to take his next breath.

"Call my mom and family; tell them to meet us there. You'll have to give her away, of course. I have a ring. Tell my mom to bring the ring my grandma gave me." He heard Phil laugh. "What's so funny? This was your idea."

"Yes, and if you fail to make her see that it's best for you both, then I'll deny it. Otherwise, I plan to take full credit. I'll call your mom in a bit. I don't think you should tell CJ. She may chicken out. I told you she tends to run when she's scared."

Austin agreed. Plus, if he pulled this off, she'd be a Force and not a Webber for real. They made plans for a little while longer. A suite with champagne and flowers, a dress for her to wear, and flowers for her wedding. They decided that the deluxe wedding would be best, Phil reading off what it entailed, and Austin told him he'd pay him for it when he saw him tomorrow.

"You're a good guy for a vamp," he told Phil before he hung up.

"Yeah, and you're an okay guy for a dog." Phil laughed. "I'll text you tomorrow when I have everything set up. Let me know when you leave and I'll make sure that everything is ready."

After hanging up, Austin crawled back into the rig with CJ and stripped down. When she didn't stir when he got into the bed with her, he pulled her soft, warm body into his and closed his eyes. This time tomorrow, she'd be his wife or he'd be a dead wolf. Smiling, he hoped he could convince her not to kill him.

CHAPTER SEVENTEEN

CJ didn't think she'd ever slept so well. Her body felt alive and humming with life when she got back in her rig after a hearty breakfast with Austin. She did notice he was acting strange, but felt much too good to let it bother her. Dressed in some very old shorts and an older T-shirt, she got behind the wheel and was off before six o'clock.

"We should be in Kingman at about five o'clock if there are no problems. We'll stop for lunch at about noon. That should take us to about the border to Nevada. There's this restaurant there called the El Rancho. Best barbeque and steaks I've ever eaten. And the place is fun too. And I need to stop at Richardson's Trading Post. I need to pick up a few more of their Navaho blankets for gifts." She flushed when Austin laughed. "Sorry. I slept really well and I was sharing."

When he reached over and pulled her in for a quick kiss when she stopped to pull into traffic, she felt her skin heat. A low growl from him made her body ache.

"If you keep growling at me like that, we'll never get there. Stop it and behave." She looked over at him when he growled again. "I mean it, Austin. You make me feel things I've never felt before."

"I'm in love with you, CJ." She jerked around to look at him, then back at the road. "I am. I know it's not what you expected…it's not even what I expected…but I do love you."

"You can't love me. I'm not…no, you just can't. Maybe it's your hormones or whatever. I'm not really the…nobody loves me."

She wanted to tell him that her own father hadn't, but then why should he? She wanted to tell him that she'd been alone for nearly all her life, and that too made her not loveable. She glanced over at him when he chuckled. He was just horny, that was all, and decided that he would get over it soon.

They were driving down the road when she noticed that he seemed to be very busy with his phone. She didn't ask, but she wanted to. If he loved her like he said, he'd want to share, she thought.

He loved her. That thought kept her mind busy. Why? That was the real question. Why would anyone in their right mind love her? It was the sex, that was all. Nothing more.

"Tell me what you're thinking about." His command had her blurt out what she had been thinking before she could stop it. "So you think it's only the sex. Okay, I can see that. You are a very sensual and sexy woman. But for me, it's much more. You make me want to be a better man."

She snorted before commenting. "Sure I do. You're the bossiest man I know. And opinionated. But why do you think you love me?"

He looked out the window before answering. "I love you because you're the most beautiful, amazing woman I know. Even knowing that what you're doing can get you hurt, you still do it. Even knowing that you've been lied to by your best friend, you've already forgiven him and didn't turn him away. I love you for your sense of humor, your laughter, and I love you because you are brilliant and stand up to me."

She didn't know what to say to that so she said nothing. He turned in his seat again and leaned against the window as she drove. When his phone rang, a tone she knew to be his brother's, she felt relieved when he went to the sleeper to use the computer. Pulling out her phone's headset, she called Phil.

"Austin said he loved me," was her greeting when he answered. She found she wished she'd called anyone else but him when he laughed. "I don't think it's the least bit funny, you jerk."

"Why wouldn't he love you? I do, and I have excellent taste." She snorted again. "You don't think I have good taste, or you don't believe I love you?"

"Both. Why? I don't understand why anyone would love me. He said all this stuff about making him laugh and that…well, other stuff too, but why? Is that a reason to love someone?"

He was quiet for a few seconds and she thought she'd lost the connection. But when he spoke, his voice was low and very emotional. She felt tears fill her eyes.

"The first time I saw you, you were on campus. I wasn't a student there, but as soon as I saw this little kid from nowhere struggling to make it across campus alone, I figured I'd found an easy target. Yeah, I had you tagged for a good lay and some food. Little did I know you'd capture my heart. You've been my protector and my friend for longer than anyone I've known. And CJ, when you live as long as I have, that's saying a lot." She wiped at the tears as he continued. "Now, why do you love me?"

"Because you made me feel protected and important to you." It hit her as suddenly as that. "Oh God, Phil, I'm in love with a werewolf."

For the most part, Austin stayed in the back. CJ was glad about that. It gave her time to think and to wonder. There were no guidelines to judge how much "in love" someone could be with another person. She just knew that every time she thought of Austin, she got all warm and fuzzy inside. When he finally came up to the front as they were pulling into Gallup, she glanced over at him.

"Okay, so I guess I love you too. I'm not sure why yet, but I can't think of any way of not loving you." His laughter made her feel stupid. "I don't think this is funny, asshole. You tricked me."

"Tricked you how? You know what, I don't care. I love you too. Now. What are we going to do about it?" She didn't know what he meant, and pulled into a space just to the left of the restaurant.

"I'm hungry. I'm going to shop for an hour and then eat a huge steak and baked potato. If you want to come along then go ahead." She was out of the rig before he answered. When he took her hand as she was entering the shop, she couldn't help but feel good.

The weather was really warm but dry. She felt the cooling air conditioning as soon as they entered. When she let go of Austin's hand and started forward, his hand touched the bare of her back. The shirt she had on today wasn't nearly as skimpy as the one from last night, but just as cool. She felt her nipples pucker and pulled the fabric away when she noticed Austin looking.

"I can't help it. It's cooler in here. You want me to go around in fur coats and baggy pants?"

"If I thought it would make you less sexy then I'd say yes. But even if you donned a gunny sack and a bag over your head, I'd still want you. Just stay close to me. I don't think you'll be able to come back here if I have to kill anyone."

She felt his compliment all the way to her toes. Trying to ignore him trying to block her from other men, she enjoyed finding presents for everyone. When she was trying to decide on which blanket to get, she turned to ask him and noticed someone staring at them.

"He's a wolf. He recognizes my scent and yours. Don't pay any attention to him unless he approaches," Austin told her when she pointed him out. "He's trying to decide if he can take you from me."

She looked up at him to see if he was kidding and realized he wasn't. She looked back over at the...boy really, and decided there was no contest. She nearly said as much to Austin when the boy came closer.

CJ wasn't sure what she had expected. Fur to sprout all over them both? A bloody fight to the death? But she was disappointed when all Austin did was pull her closer and growl at the kid. He moved away from them so quickly she thought it was sad.

"Well, that was quick. Do you think your sister will like the blue one or the brown one?" She looked up at him when he still held her and he hadn't answered. "What is it?"

"I want you to finish up and go to the rig. This isn't over. Do as I say, CJ. I won't have you hurt because some young pup thinks he can kick my ass." She looked back at the door and saw the boy standing just outside with another young man. "He won't leave until it's done."

"You mean you'll kill him." She looked up at him and saw the determined look on his face. "Christ, you do mean to kill him. He's just a boy."

CJ shoved the things they'd picked out into his arms. She walked straight to the boy and his friends and smacked him across the mouth. She could hear Austin cussing right behind her. The kid looked at her while he rubbed his mouth.

"What the fuck was that for?" the kid next to him snarled with a step toward her. She drew back and slapped him too.

"You'll watch your mouth, young man." She looked at the kid she'd slapped first. "Did that hurt?"

"Yeah, you want me to show you?" She drew back her hand again and he took a step back. "Are you nuts?"

"So it hurt. Good. Now tell me, what do you think that the man behind me would have done to you? Less? More?" She knew Austin was right behind her, but he didn't say anything. "I want you to take a good look at him and tell me truthfully what you think would have happened."

The boy looked over her shoulder and then took a step back. "He probably would have killed me."

"Austin?" She hoped he'd be honest with her and do what she wanted.

"Oh yeah, he'd be a dead pup. Might still be if he doesn't show my mate more respect." CJ nearly burst out laughing at both boys' faces. "You got a name, kid?" She held her breath. She was afraid from the resentful look on his face they would be smart-alecky. But with a quick glance over at the other boy, the first one answered.

"I'm Reid Atkins and that's my brother Randy. We...we didn't mean no harm, ma'am." He looked over her shoulder again and moved forward slowly, putting out his hand. "I'm sorry, sir. I didn't mean to mess up your day."

When he walked closer to her, she could see that he was too thin. She could also see that his clothes were ill fitting and that he needed a bath. She looked at the other boy and saw the same thing. Before she could say anything, Austin did.

"You hungry?" Reid looked over at his brother before nodding. "Come inside with us and help me carry my mate's purchases to the truck. When we're done, we'll get some lunch and talk."

She didn't speak as she went around all three of them. She didn't know what Austin had done with her things until she saw them piled up on the counter. CJ smiled at the clerk and asked her if she could continue shopping and leave the items there. Of course, the woman was thrilled to help out.

Austin came up behind her when she was looking at some western shirts. When he wrapped his arm around her waist, she leaned back on him. She could feel his laughter.

"I'm not sure if I should kiss you or beat your ass. Christ, don't ever do anything like that again. They could have hurt you." He stepped back when she heard someone clear his or her throat. "You boys are to find you some clothes. Three shirts each, and two pair of jeans. Don't be stupid and try and tell me you don't need them."

While they went to the men's department, CJ looked up at Austin. "Do they have somewhere to go, you think? They look like they haven't eaten in weeks."

"No. They don't. And you're probably right." He looked at her before he spoke. "You probably saved their lives...you know that, right?"

She hugged him to her. "You wouldn't have hurt them."

When they made it to the restaurant, CJ had only one bag. The rest was being shipped home. The boys had several pairs of jeans each and three shirts. They ended up getting jackets and some other things as well. By the time they were seated, an extra hour later than she wanted, the boys and Austin were getting along well. She knew he was making arrangements with his brother to pick them up at the airport tomorrow afternoon.

"You piss my brother off and you piss me off. If you can't follow rules then I'll punish you in ways you can't imagine. Understand me?" Austin seemed pleased that he'd increased his pack by two, and the boys were thrilled to have someone helping them. She only hoped the pack could afford to feed them. She'd never seen anyone pack away food the way they did.

The cab that picked them up and took them to the hotel met them near the rig. Austin gave them each fifty dollars to eat that night and for breakfast in the morning. The hotel would make sure they had a way to the airport. They were being met by Dallas in Ohio and set up in a new pack. The boys had taken on more than they could chew, she thought, and had come out the winners.

Austin went to the back of the rig and she followed him. She wanted to show him what she'd bought, but he had other things in mind. He told her that she was going to be punished for running head long into a situation that could have gotten her hurt.

CHAPTER EIGHTEEN

"You most certainly are not going to spank me. I'm a grown woman and I won't do it." CJ hadn't moved from where she stood since he'd told her he was going to spank her.

Austin started taking off his belt. He wasn't going to use it on her, but the look in her eyes made him think she might use it on him. When he unbuttoned his jeans, she licked her lips.

"I said take off your pants. You're not making this any easier on yourself by delaying the inevitable. You walked foolhardily into something that, lucky for them, turned out well. But I won't have you doing that again." She crossed her arms over her chest and glared at him. "CJ, I'm not playing around here."

"Well that's good, because neither am I. You are not, and I repeat not, going to spank me." She tried to dodge his hand when he grabbed for her, but he was quicker. She fought like a hell cat or a pissed off bitch. He held her until she calmed.

"You could have been hurt today. You can't scare me like that." He kissed her neck. "I have to make you realize that you can't do that again."

"Please don't do this. I'll make you regret it if you do." She backed her ass up against his hardening erection as she continued. "For a very, very long time."

He reached up, cupped her breast in his palm, and pinched her nipple. "Then what do you suggest I do? I can't let you get by with this sort of behavior."

The need to punish her was fast becoming a need to fuck her. He rocked into her ass again when she didn't answer right away. He could smell her need and wondered fleetingly if he'd ever tire of her. Never, he decided quickly. Never would he not need her.

"I'll do…you name it, and I'll do it. Just don't spank me and I'll do whatever you want me to, no questions asked."

Austin paused. "Anything?"

"Yes. I promise you. You ask me, and it's as good as done." She turned in his arms. "Deal?"

"Marry me. Tomorrow you will go to Vegas with me and marry me." Her face paled and he thought she would say no, but she nodded once and pulled away.

He climbed into the passenger seat as she put the keys in the ignition. He reached over, took them out, and held them. She didn't move.

"I need those," she said quietly. "Please give them to me. We're running behind now. I can't—"

"My family is already there. So is Phil. I planned this yesterday when I found out that we'd only be two hours from there." She looked at him then. "My mom is bringing the ring I want you to wear and that has been in my family for generations. Reid and Randy aren't going back to Ohio. They're taking a plane to Vegas too, and Dallas and Phil are meeting them at the airport. I have booked us the honeymoon suite, with champagne in the room when we arrive."

She turned back to the steering wheel and looked out the front. She was very still, very quiet for a long while, and he knew she was thinking. He let her. He didn't want her to think the only reason he was going to marry her was because she didn't want to get a spanking.

"Your mom, what does she think about you marrying me? She can't be thrilled." He could hear the doubt in her voice and wanted to pull her into his arms and tell her he loved her, but knew that she needed this right now.

"No, she's not thrilled. But not about you marrying me. She's upset because we're not having a wedding at home where she can plan it. She likes you. And so does Holly. Dallas thinks you're getting a bum deal, and my brothers are looking forward to kissing the bride."

Austin saw the tear run down her cheek and he said her name softly. "I love you very much, CJ. More than I thought possible. I never meant to hurt you, but you scared me. Also, when you did that, all I could think of was how proud I was of you, how wonderful of an alpha bitch you're—"

"Bitch? I don't think so. You'll have to come up with another name or I will be a bitch." His heart pounded at her words. "Another thing, if you think this will get you out of your trying to spank me in the future, you're nuts. Now give me the keys. We have to make five hours tonight."

He called his brother first. He'd been talking to him since the boys had told him that they were on their own. He wanted to make sure the boys were picked up at the airport and that they were cleaned up when he and CJ got to Vegas that night.

Reid said that the last pack they had belonged to had shunned them because their mother was barren. They seemed to think that the boys, a product of a rape from the alpha, would be as well. They had been on their own for over four years. Attacking Austin was just a way to lift his wallet. CJ had been correct in assuming they hadn't eaten in some time.

"I have a room set up for them, and a guy is coming in to fit them with suits." Dallas hesitated before continuing. "Are you sure about this? What if they just trade in their tickets and take your money?"

Austin had thought of that too. "They might, but if they do then they'll be stupider than I thought. They have money to eat on the way there. The pilot said he'd make sure there was food and drink on board for them, and he'd make sure to call me if they didn't show. But I don't think they'll skip out. They reminded me of us when we were growing up...all legs and arms."

Dallas snorted. "Sure, and when they get here what's to stop them from murdering us in the night? For all you know they could be a couple of con artists and you fell for it."

"If they give you any shit, tell them CJ will hurt them." Austin told his brother what happened at the shop. "I think they're terrified of her."

Dallas roared with laughter. "Christ, she's going to be a hell of an alpha bitch. I can't wait to see her in action at the next lunar gathering. She will have them in line in no time."

"Yeah, probably. But you might want to not call her a bitch. She gets a might pissy about it. She told me that she wants us to come up with another name. I think I'll work on that." Austin changed the subject when he looked over at CJ. "That guy called us last night. I had CJ tell him to meet us at the warehouse because she didn't know anyone in the company. He's going to meet us there. I was wondering if you could come along? Maybe for a ride and nothing more."

"I'd be glad to. You never know what might happen, and I'd never forgive myself if anything happened to CJ." Dallas laughed again. "Seriously, I want to be there and was going to ask. Phil wants to be there as well. We were actually thinking we'd leave tonight and be there when you guys arrive."

Austin told CJ and she agreed. He wouldn't normally ask anyone for advice on things, but she was his mate and he wanted her beside him, not trying to protect him like she had that day. He hung up with his brother after a few more minutes and leaned back in the chair. She really had scared him.

When she'd shoved the things into his arms, he thought she was going to go straight to the rig and wondered how he was going to get the things to her before he kicked some ass. When he saw her slap the first one then the second, he'd nearly shifted and went after them. By the time he got to them after throwing everything on the counter and telling the woman to stay, he realized she not only had things under control, but she also had the boys eating out of her hand.

"How does one convert?" Her question brought him out of his thoughts. "I mean, to a wolf?"

"I would have to bite you, deep and hard, and I'd hold my teeth into you so that my essences would go into your blood stream." He didn't want to think about having to hurt her like that, but he wanted her as his true mate.

"But you said the bite you gave me wouldn't change me. What has to be different?" She glanced over at him. "There's more than that, isn't there?"

"Yes. Trauma...there would have to be several bites at first...deep ones in the fleshy part of your body that would be extremely painful. Then I would bite you at your neck or another place where there is a major vein or artery, and hold you that way until I felt the change coming on." He took a deep breath before he told her the last part. "I would have to be a wolf, a full wolf, for me to change you."

Austin watched her for any sign of revulsion. She stared out the window and frowned. He didn't have to wait long before she figured it out.

"You don't really want to do it, do you? You don't want to hurt me."

He looked out his window before answering her. "No. No I don't. I want you to be my mate in all ways, but the thought of...." He shuddered before going on. "The thought of causing you so much pain sickens me."

He'd seen a female human go through it once. She'd been smaller than CJ and a lot less healthy. She'd been in a bad way for a long time from one thing or another, and had wanted to change to be with her brother, who had been changed because of a fight. Austin could still hear her screams and see the terror on her face when the wolf, her brother, had come toward her.

Her brother hadn't done his job in changing her. He'd not bitten hard enough or held her down long enough to let the change begin. The female had died and the brother had left the pack and never returned. Austin had heard that he'd hung himself.

"I'm afraid to do it." He watched her as her hand reached for his. "You could stay with me as my mate. I could live with that."

She held his hand and said nothing. The next few hours went by slowly for him. The traffic got heavier the closer they got to Kingman, where they parked. Austin saw the limo before they got out of the rig. Three men from another pack had been assigned to watch the rig until they returned the next day. Austin made a mental note to thank his brother.

~~~

The wedding was a simple affair. Nancy had wanted it to be at home with the pack around, but was glad her son had found someone so worthy of him. She doubted that either of them realized how much they suited each other. Nancy already liked CJ, and was thrilled when the others did as well.

"I want to kiss the bride first. You can kiss the next bride first."

Nancy nearly yelled at her sons when she saw that CJ had it under control.

"If you two want to fight then go to your rooms. This is a nice place, and you guys acting like children isn't going to be tolerated." CJ glared at them both before she continued in a calming voice. "Now, we'll settle this like adults, or no one gets to kiss the bride."

"How we going to do that?" Connor asked. He looked at her like she was going to tell him the cure to some major problem. "Can't both of us kiss you first?"

"No, you can't. But you can kiss me first on the right and left cheek...one on one side, the other on the other side. Then later when I get back to Ohio, you can trade places...provided you don't piss me off again."

Nancy nearly burst out laughing when her sons got on either side of CJ. She thought there was going to be trouble when they couldn't agree on which side was better until CJ simply walked away. They made their decision quickly and without a single argument. And they each got to kiss the bride.

Nancy looked over at the two young men Dallas had picked up at the airport that afternoon. Her heart went out to them for what they had endured. Neither of them had had an easy life, and she could see that they adored CJ. Nancy didn't even question how they had come to be a part of the wedding party, but knew that however it happened, they would be well cared for in her son's pack. Looking over at her son and his new bride, she saw the vampire sitting well away from the others.

Phil Campbell was a good man too, she realized, and he loved CJ. But there was nothing there for anyone to be upset about. Austin and the older man seemed to be good friends, and anyone could see that Phil would do anything for Austin and CJ. That's when she noticed her daughter.

Holly seemed to be apart from everyone too. While she watched, she had a thought and then another. When all the pieces fell into place, she nearly laughed out loud. Mates—Phil and Holly were mates, and both of them seemed to know it. She watched them for a bit longer when she realized something else. CJ knew it too.

CHAPTER NINETEEN

The room was lovely. CJ walked around and touched all the things that made the room look homey. She didn't, of course, go near the bed, but she did look at the bathroom and the large living room area twice. When Austin chuckled, she turned to glare at him.

"You finished searching the room now or do you want to have another go? I'm sure there are a couple of things you might have missed the second time."

"I was just admiring the decorations." She hoped he wouldn't ask her which ones, because as soon as she looked at him again, every thought went out of her head.

Christ, he was beautiful. The tux that his mom had brought for him fit like a glove…a very sexy, very big glove. She wanted to go to him, strip him slowly, and kiss each and every inch she exposed.

"CJ, you keep looking at me like that and all my good intentions to make slow love to you in that bed are going to fly away." He took a step toward her and she held up her hand to stop him.

"I want to touch you. I want to take your clothes off you and taste you. Can I do that, Austin? Will you let me explore you and you not touch me?" Her voice had gotten husky, so husky she barely recognized it as her own.

When he nodded to her, she moved forward and started to unbutton his shirt. She kissed the first bit of his furred chest. He was warm and hard and wonderfully delicious.

"I never get to see much of you when we have sex." She opened the shirt more and found his nipple. She wondered if it was as sensitive as hers were. She ran her tongue over the pebbled bit of flesh and moaned when he hissed at her.

"Because you drive me insane with need when I touch you."

She looked up at him as she circled around behind him and reached for his jacket. "Maybe. Or you just need to be inside of me that badly." The jacket came off and she laid it over the chair. "I don't know if you realize this or not, but this is the first time we've been in a real bed together. I'm looking forward to riding you like I did that day on the seat." His growl made her pussy gush. "I love that sound you make. Do you have any idea what it does to me to hear you growl like a big animal? I nearly come when I hear it."

She knew she was pushing it, but she was having too much fun not to. When she came around to the front of him again, she could see that she was arousing him more than she thought she could.

This time, she stepped back. She could barely stand on her own two feet and thought that she'd have him do the rest. She sat on the edge of the bed and crooked her finger at him. "Come here, Austin. I want to take your cock in my mouth and suck you until you come." She never saw him move. One minute he was standing in the middle of the room, the next she was pressed against the bed and he was all over her.

"You drive me nuts, woman. I can't decide if I want you to ride me or suck me. Christ, you'll kill me before morning." He moved to the edge of the bed and stood. "Watch me strip for you. Then when I'm naked, you'll do the same for me. I want to watch you peel away that beautiful dress and show me what my sister bought for you to wear under it." He wiggled his brows at her. "Or I could strip you bare and find out all on my own."

She smiled when she thought of what she had on...or what she didn't have on. There was a tiny scrap of lace that fit over her pussy and then a few strings. She'd not put on a bra; the dress had one built in. And the stockings, thigh-highs, with heels Holly had called "fuck me" heels. But it was the dress that made her smile.

It was simply the most beautiful thing she'd ever seen, and it was his mom's. Nancy told her that she'd been saving it forever for one of the boys' wives to use, and never dreamed it would fit so well. The creamy white lace that covered her bodice and arms looked fragile and sexy. The rest of the dress, covered in the same lace, lay over a waterfall of silk and fell to the floor in yards and yards of white. The dress molded over her curves like it had been painted on them and the hips flared out enough to hide the slit up each side that showed off her long legs. She moved one of those now to show Austin what she had beneath.

"Silk stockings are expensive, and you'll have a care with this dress, thank you very much. I won't have you tearing your mom's dress after she was kind enough to lend it to me."

"Then you best take it off yourself, wife, for I have a need to fuck you hard." His words had her wet, hot, and oh so ready for him to do just that. "Watch me, CJ. Watch me undress for you."

The cummerbund came off next. He took it off with such a flourish that she felt her breath hitch. Next came the shirt. She'd already opened most of the buttons so it was just a matter of him pulling it free of his pants and taking it off. But he only finished the buttons and then went to his belt.

He took his time now, sliding the tab out of the small eye, pulling it free of the loop. She watched his fingers as they did each movement, worked the leather from the cinch, guided it through the loops of the pants. By the time it hit the floor with his cummerbund, she was soaking wet and panting.

"Do you have any idea what it's doing to me to smell you right now? How much I want to strip off my pants and throw you over and pound deep into you?" She shook her head, not able to speak from the dryness of her throat. "My cock aches to be inside of you. My wolf, always on the surface when you smell like sex, is snarling at me to free him so that he can fuck you too."

"Will he?" She cleared her throat to try again. "Will you allow him to take me, Austin?"

He paused in the process of opening the button at his pants. "Would you like that? Would you like for him to take you? When the moon is full and you're my wolf, I'll let him. He'll take you from behind and hold you still with his teeth deep in your shoulder. He'll take you hard and fill you with his cum."

"Austin, please. You need to hurry. I'm so wet and needy for you." She lay back on the bed. Lifting the dress up, she showed him her wet panties. His growl made her bold and she ran her fingers over the tiny lace that held it over her pussy.

"Touch yourself. Slide your fingers into your panties and deep into your heat." His voice was hard, rough, and low. She could no more not do as he commanded than stop breathing. "That's it. Christ, you're beautiful."

She watched him strip off his clothes, quicker now as she touched her clit. It was hard and slick, and when she brushed her finger over it, she moaned. When he stood her up suddenly, she moaned when her fingers were jerked free. But when he took them to his mouth and suckled them, she felt her knees buckle.

"Strip. Take the dress off now or I will shred it. I've lost my ability to be gentle." He turned her around and started on the buttons. There were nearly one hundred of them, Nancy told her, and all them had to be sewn back on after her wedding night.

"Your mother said your father scattered the buttons around the room. She said it took her hours to find them all. If you help me find them—" She never finished as she felt the dress open and buttons fell around her feet.

The dress pooled to the floor and his hands tore the panties from her. When he turned her around, she was as naked as him. But he didn't touch her. He stepped back and looked.

"You are simply the most beautiful creature I've ever seen. Your breasts fill my hands and your nipples fill my mouth." He gently lifted them in the palms of his hands, leaned down, and suckled each nipple before letting her go. "You waist is so small that I can wrap my fingers around you and nearly touch, but you aren't tiny." He did as he said and wrapped his warm hands around her, then moved them to her hips. "Hips I can fill my hands with, hold onto when I enter you. When I take your ass, and I will, it will cradle my cock deep and hold me to you. Your legs are strong and long, and I love the feel of them when you wrap them around me."

He dropped to his knees and slid his fingers up her thighs. She could feel him gather the cream that had leaked from her. His moan as he ran his tongue up the same path made her tremble. His fingers sliding into her pussy brought her to a quick climax, soft and breathtaking.

"That's only the beginning. I plan to take you to peak all night long. You belong to me now, and I'll make sure you never forget it." He pulled her to him and suckled her clit into his mouth.

~~~

She flooded his mouth with her juices. When he slid his fingers into her heat, his hand soaked and cream ran down his arm. Lapping her, he could feel her legs shake and he wanted her to collapse, wanted her to scream out her release until she was hoarse.

Her climax was building and he pushed her over the edge by nipping gently at her clit. Her fingers in his hair tightened and he heard her cry out. Standing up, he lifted her in his arms and took her to the chair.

"Lean over it and brace your hands on the arms. I'm going to play back here and I want you in the position to take me." She looked dazed and he showed her what he wanted from her. "You've no idea what it does to me to see you like this."

He opened her legs wider and saw her pussy. Rubbing the head of his cock, coating it with her wetness, he slid slowly into her. His movements were slow and easy, just enough to keep them both on edge.

"Austin, please. Fuck me before I have to kill you." He smacked her ass, and when she started to rise up, he held her in place with his hand. "What the hell do you think you're doing? Let me go."

"No. You're going to stay right here." He brought his hand down on her ass again, then again. "You should see what I'm doing to your ass. It's pink with my hand print."

"I can feel it and it's not turning me on right now. Stop that or else." When he smacked her again, he heard her moan. "Austin, please."

"You like it, I can tell. Your sheath tightens around me every time I burn your ass." He reached around her and ran his fingers into her pussy. "You're so wet, baby. I'm going to fuck you and make you come, then I'm going to work your ass for my cock."

He rubbed her juices around her ass, then parted her cheeks and rubbed his thumb over the tiny puckered rosette. Over and over he rubbed his thumb over her until she started to back up into it. When he broke through the tight muscles, she tightened around his cock.

With his thumb deep in her ass, he grabbed her hip with his free hand and started to fuck her hard. His thumb moved in and out to the rhythm he was pounding into her until he felt her following him every time he pulled out of her pussy. When she came, she nearly strangled his cock and brought him with her.

He couldn't move. He wasn't in a hurry to do so, but he did kiss her back as he leaned over her. She tasted of sex and sweat, a sweet combination that made him want more of her. Standing, he pulled free of her body, picked her up in his arms, and took her to the bed.

As soon as he lay down beside her, she rolled over him and tucked her head beneath his chin. Reaching down with the last of his strength, he pulled the blankets over them and closed his eyes. His last thoughts before sleep claimed him were that she was his for good now.

~~~

Austin moved against the heat. His cock felt warm, hard, and enveloped in hot wetness. When he opened his eyes he looked down, and saw the most beautiful sight he'd ever seen. CJ had her body wedged against his and her mouth around his cock.

His fingers were already tangled in her hair and he was riding her mouth when he came fully awake. When she cupped his balls and tugged gently at them, he nearly came up off the bed.

"Baby, please. If you keep that up, I'm going to come down your throat. And as much as I'd like to do that, you mentioned riding me." She let him go with a small pop. "Come here. Sit on my face. I want to taste what sucking me did to you."

She scrambled up his body and moved her thighs on either side of his face. Heaven was all he could think, and paradise was just a lick away. Wrapping his hands around her legs, he pulled her down and took her.

"Austin," she screamed, and his mouth was flooded with her release. "I need you. Please," she begged as she rode his mouth. "Please, I need your cock inside of me."

Lifting her up, he moved her down his chest and over his groin. She was leaning down to take his nipple into her mouth when he sat her down over his straining cock. Sitting her up, he growled at her to ride.

It didn't take either of them long to come. She set up a brutal pace and he leaned up and took her pert nipple in his mouth. When she cupped her breasts and fed him, he pulled her harder over him and surged up into her with every downward stroke.

"Come. Come now," he commanded, and she came apart. Rolling her to her back, he rocked into her heat once, twice, then a third time and roared out his own release. Throwing back his head, he howled, something he'd not done since he'd been a teenager in the throes of climax his first time.

CHAPTER TWENTY

Wayne looked at the marquee for twenty-five minutes, waiting for it to come back around to the name he never dreamed of seeing there. When it came back on, "Congratulations Mr. & Mrs. Austin and CJ Force," he nearly jumped up and down. Instead, he looked over at Arthur.

They had flown into Vegas just over an hour ago. They were going to meet a new buyer for the merchandise in the truck that was coming across the States in three days. The stuff CJ was carrying was going directly to Arthur's stores to be sold to all those fools who wanted to have a Merry Christmas. *Suckers*, was all that Wayne could think.

"She's here." At Arthur's confused look, he explained. "CJ Webber, now Force, is here in Vegas. Which means our merchandise is. Seems her and her rider just got married."

Arthur smiled. "Well isn't that just great? Maybe we should make our acquaintance with our driver. Where is she staying?"

Wayne told him which marquee he'd read it on and they had the driver of the limo turn around and head back toward the hotel. They were checked in less than twenty minutes later.

There were a number of wedding suites in the hotel. Most of them were occupied, Wayne found out when he told the clerk at the desk that his daughter was at the church getting married right now. Mary, the very helpful clerk, told him that three couples were checking out that day and that by noon their rooms would be ready. He booked one of the rooms and asked to see it. He was just getting off the elevator when he saw CJ come out of the room and push a tray out into the hall. Room twelve-seventeen, his new favorite number. With a quick look around a room that wouldn't be used, he got back into the elevator and went down three floors to his own room.

He wanted her. He could smell the wolf all over her, but that didn't stop him from wanting to crawl between her legs and sate his lust. He freed his swollen cock and stroked it while he thought of all the things he was going to do to the bitch. Before he could come, there was a knock at his door. Snarling out a string of curse words, he yanked the door open without even putting his cock back into his pants.

"Are you alone or just playing with yourself? Come on," Arthur said with disgust in his voice. "I'm wanting dinner and I don't want to eat alone. And wash your fucking hands. Masturbating is a sin, you know."

Wayne would have laughed, but he thought if he did he might have to shoot the man. He was reasonably sure that murder and stealing were sins as well, but Arthur seemed to have no problem with those two. Wayne slammed the door and walked over to the bar as he did up his pants. His hard-on was gone anyway now that he'd had to deal with his boss.

"We just going to walk up to her and tell her who we are, or do you have a plan?" Wayne poured himself three fingers of bourbon and a glass of sherry for the man behind him. "I'm sure the man with her is a wolf, but not much in the food chain, I think. If he were, he'd not let his bitch drive across country like she did."

"Hmm, I believe you might be right. I could smell him on the truck that night, but not much more than he was a wolf. They were having a conversation, and since the steel of the truck prevented me from actually hearing, I didn't know what was going on."

Wayne had been pissed when he found out that Arthur knew where the girl and the merchandise was. Apparently, he'd stuck a tracer on the trailer before it left the lot at the warehouse in Ohio. He told Wayne that he'd be stupid not to know where the truck was when he wanted to steal it. He'd followed her...or had until sometime late yesterday when the signal stopped. Arthur had found the fragments of it in Arizona, where it had probably fallen off the truck.

"As for a plan," Arthur continued. "Yes, I have one. I think we should simply take the merchandise from her and then her. I don't know who you were thinking about just now, but I've seen the girl, and I for one would like a good taste of her before we have to get rid of her."

Wayne felt his wolf roll with anger. He wanted her for himself. He turned to look at Arthur and could see that his beast, a weretiger, was just on the surface as well. Now they had a problem. If either of them shifted, one of them was going to die. And Wayne had no intentions of it being him.

Arthur reached for the glass and Wayne could see the fur on his hand. He was closer than he thought. Letting his own wolf pour through just a little, he could feel his beast snarl for blood. Holding him back gently, telling him that he'd have his taste, he looked at Arthur.

"She's mine." Arthur stood as Wayne spoke. "You touch her and I'll rip you apart."

The shift of man to tiger was amazing. One second two men were talking and the next, a vicious, large, orange and black tiger was snarling at him. Wayne let his beast go and felt the power that came with him.

He felt the tears to his flesh, the pain of it. But he also felt more, the taste of blood, hot and full of hate. He tasted his adversary's pain and the wonderful staggering power of it. Wayne knew how to fight; he knew how to tear into muscle and bone. He loved the feeling of breaking ribs, getting to the heart, the blood pounding heart, of one he planned to kill.

Wayne swiped his claws over the tiger's throat, deep and visceral, and felt the splash of blood as it shot from the jugular. His roar of triumph was loud even as the tiger tried to fend him off. But he could taste the victory, could taste the man's dying even as the tiger did. When he shifted back from wolf, Wayne got the pleasure of seeing Arthur take his last breath as a man, his last light fading from his eyes as he knew he was dying.

"She's mine." Wayne kicked Arthur in the ribs for good measure. Then he looked at the carnage of the room.

Very little of it remained whole. The couch and chair that were in the once lovely suite now lay in tatters, the stuffing and fine leather now in bits all over the room and covered in blood. The table that had two chairs around it now was nothing more than splintered wood. Liquor from the bar and the broken glass lay strewn about the floor like a Jackson Pollack painting gone mad. The blood from the naked man on the floor stained the pale carpet and filled the room with the scent of bloodlust. Drapes at the closed curtains hung in long strips of material, letting in the hot morning sunlight and heat. Wayne smiled, thinking he wished he could see the face of the cleaning staff when they came to clear this mess.

Going to one of the bedrooms, he grabbed the comforter off the bed and brought it back to the dead man. With as much flourish as he could muster for the bastard, Wayne covered him, then walked to his own bedroom to shower. He stopped in mid-step, went to the door, put out the "do not disturb" sign, and went to wash away the blood and sweat.

Feeling refreshed and energized, Wayne made his way to the elevator and to the lobby. He decided that he'd get the girl, take her to the truck, and fuck her. She'd probably enjoy that after a night with a lesser wolf. He wished fleetingly that he'd made an effort to see what the other wolf looked like, but let the thought go. Wayne knew that as an alpha, he'd be far superior to the lesser wolf, and sat down in the lobby to wait. He saw her striding toward the gift shop not five minutes later.

~~~

CJ made her way to the gift shop. She'd had a call from the desk telling her that the wedding pictures they'd taken yesterday were finished and ready to be picked up. Austin wanted her to wait, but she left the room anyway. She was just going into the large shop when someone came up behind her. Before she could react, she heard a voice she'd thought was still in Ohio.

"You'll come with me and I won't kill you. I mean to have what belongs to me, and you are going to be a part of it." He licked her neck and she cringed. "You do that now, but later when you're beneath me you'll be singing a different tune, I'll wager."

"Doubtful. I just got married. I don't suppose I can convince you to let me go, can I? I would hate to have my husband rip your head from your shoulders." She shrugged before continuing. "Not that I really care, but you might."

That earned her a quick cuff to the head. She could see a few stars from it, but it didn't really hurt overly much. She grinned when she realized this guy thought she was afraid of him.

"Come on. We're going to my car…I don't have a car. Fuck, we came here in a limo. Now what?"

"Maybe you should have planned better, moron. Let me go and I won't hurt you. You have got to be the dumbest kidnapper I've ever heard of." She knew he couldn't do overly much to her in the crowded lobby, but she thought she might have gone just a tad too far when he punched her head against the wall. "Fucker, that hurt. You are so going to pay for that."

She saw Austin get off the elevator. As he came toward her, she shook her head. He had to see the blood on her head, but she didn't want him to get hurt. As he got closer, she could see that he wasn't just upset, but royally pissed off. When he saw who was holding her, he stopped.

"Let her go and nobody gets hurt." Austin's voice was deceptively calm, she knew this. But she wanted him to leave so he wouldn't get hurt.

"I already tried that," she told him. "He seems to think he and I are going to make love or some shit and that I'll enjoy it. He doesn't seem to think you were up to par. I don't understand where he'd get information like that. Is there a werewolf web site that grades you guys on performance?"

"No, but if you want, you and I can set one up. What would you rate me on a scale of—?"

"Shut the fuck up," Solomon snarled. "Shut the fuck up and listen to me. I'm taking her and her mate won't know…who are you anyway? Her mate's alpha?"

"No, dipshit, he is my mate. And an alpha. Oh look, his…I always forget what he's called. Must be because this turd,"—she jerked her head to Solomon—"keeps bobbing my head against the wall. Forgetfulness."

Austin turned his head and looked before turning back to her. "Enforcer, love. He's my enforcer. I'll make you a chart to learn all the different branches."

The banter was making her giggle. But she also noticed that Austin was making his way closer to them. She hoped that they were distracting Solomon enough that he didn't notice. But when Dallas stood next to his brother, he wasn't so easy to play with.

"Howdy, Dallas," Austin said in an exaggerated drawl. "This man seems to think my mate should pick him over me. We were also just discussing putting up a web page to rate wolf lovers. What do you think?"

Dallas looked so confused that CJ burst out laughing, but stopped when she felt the gun poke her hard in the back. They had now drawn quite a crowd. Austin nodded to her left and she didn't have to look to know that more reinforcements had arrived.

"I want you all to back off. I'm leaving here with her and none of you are going to stop me. I'll kill her if you do. I want my merchandise and I want the girl." They took two steps back as Solomon spoke, spittle spraying from his mouth. "I want you to back off before I have to...I have to tell on you."

"Tell on him? Are you serious—?" Her head suddenly throbbed with pain. He'd hit her again with the gun. "If you fucking hit me again, I'm going to make you sorry."

"You're going to make me sorry? Oh, and how do you plan to do that?" Solomon said as he waved the gun around the crowd of people. "You think I won't shoot these people and blame it all on you?"

One had to love Vegas people. They were watching this man waving a gun around them, a bloodied person in his arms, and not one of them came to help her. She supposed they were playing it safe, but what the hell? Then she noticed a camera or two. Okay, maybe they thought this was a movie or something.

CJ had had enough. "Like this, asshole."

She brought her foot down hard on his instep. His howl of pain had him tightening his grip on her arm. CJ felt the flesh of her forearm sort of tear. She tossed her head back, hoping to break his nose, but it at the very least made him let her go. The gun going off made her flinch, but before she could recover, she was suddenly on the ground and free. As she tried to turn over, she watched Austin tear into Solomon.

CJ watched in fascinated horror as Austin did a partial shift. His hands became clawed weapons and his jaw morphed into a scary version of the wolf from Little Red Riding Hood. All she needed was a cape and a basket and the scene would be complete.

She felt hands on her, but she couldn't hear anything. She looked up into the face of Dallas and while she was sure he was speaking, she couldn't for the life of her figure it out…something about blood and ambulance. CJ looked over at Austin just as she was pressed back onto the floor…or she fell.

Her body began to burn. Well, burn would have been nice, she thought. Right now it felt as if someone had put a torch in her belly and she was going to burn from the inside out. She looked down to see if someone would put her out, and that's when she saw the blood.

"Oh God, I'm bleeding. What happened? Did I fall?" CJ lifted her hand from the bloody mess on her shirt and held it to Dallas. "Did someone hurt me?"

Other than the burning, there wasn't any pain. But that soon changed and she heard someone screaming. She wanted them to stop, but she was suddenly very lightheaded. And then she was very cold.

People were beginning to fade in and out. First there was Dallas, then Phil. She saw her mother and then her grandma, but they sort of became Nancy, then Holly. Finally, she closed her eyes, only to jerk them back open when someone said her name.

"Stay with me, sweetheart. Come on, keep your eyes open so I can make sure you're not going into shock." Phil smiled at her and she tried to smile back, but her lips quit working.

"Baby. Oh Christ. Listen to me baby. We have to get you somewhere that I can…we have to take her somewhere now." She wanted to reach up and smooth the wrinkles in Austin's forehead as he spoke, but she couldn't make her hand raise. And he was shouting again.

She started to fade out. She thought that was the perfect name for the way she was feeling…fading away. Then a stupid song popped in her head. She was humming it when she felt someone slide their hands under her.

The pain ripped through her. It made her scream and she couldn't have held back even if she'd tried. When she looked into the face of the man who held her, Austin looked as pale as a sheet. Her last thought was that he looked so afraid.

Kathi S. Barton

CHAPTER TWENTY ONE

Austin watched the nurses come and go. No one came to where they were sitting. He glanced around the room with a sardonic grin. He probably would have avoided them too.

In addition to him and his family, there were the two Adkins boys, Phil, and any number of flack-vested men and women. There were so many initials and letters across their fronts and backs that he was reminded of a chalkboard with primer letters on it. He glanced over when his mom sat beside him.

"She's strong. And the doctor said she was going to be all right. Besides, I believe she's too stubborn to die. She's pretty upset with you yet as well."

Austin burst out laughing, then hugged his mom to him. "I believe you're right. She did seem to want to tear into me when she woke up, didn't she? She seemed to be fairly pissed that she was brought here without her permission. She said I could count on her to kick my ass when she woke up." Austin wanted her to. He wanted her healthy so that she could get up and berate him for calling the ambulance. The ride to the hospital might have been funny if he'd not been so terrified out of his mind for her.

One of the agents came to stand next to him and his mom. The agent cleared his throat before speaking. Austin stood up and the man backed up two steps.

"Mr. Force, we need to ask you a few questions about what might have happened in the hotel lobby." He took another step back before he continued. "Mr. Solomon…he…we don't know what happened."

Austin didn't look at Phil, though he was sure the man could hear them speaking. But he did look at his mom, who got up and walked away after a short nod. He was sure she knew as well as he did what had happened to the man, but there was no reason to get her involved unless he had to.

"Happened? I'm not sure I understand your question. My wife was shot by Mr. Solomon, the man I believe you people had under surveillance." Austin took a step toward the man and was happy to see him back up two. "Have you arrested him yet?"

The agent, Agent Jimmie Oliver Austin thought his name was, looked like he turned green. Austin could smell the man's fear as well. It came off him in waves.

"He's dead. I…we found him…he was…destroyed." Oliver sat down abruptly and put his head between his legs as he continued. "Never in all my years have I ever…. He was torn apart. Not just, you know, his arms and legs off, but torn to pieces. Small, little bitty pieces. We found parts of him over a ten square foot area. The coroner said that the man or men who…whoever did this didn't use a knife or a blade, but simply ripped him apart."

Austin did look at Phil then, and the man winked then saluted him. Austin sat down and pressed his hand over his mouth to keep from bursting out into laughter. It wasn't funny that the other man was dead. It was just funny to see Phil so casual about it.

When Austin had seen CJ drop to the floor in the hotel lobby, he'd only looked away from Solomon for a second, maybe less. Then he was simply gone. When Austin went to CJ's side, Phil was gone suddenly, then he was there again as Austin carried CJ to the lobby area and put her on one of the couches.

Before he could ask Phil where he'd gone, where Solomon had gone, a doctor had come forward and started working on CJ. The ambulance was pulling up when CJ came around.

"What's going on? Austin? Phil?" CJ looked confused until she looked down at herself. "Oh Christ, I'm bleeding. That fat bastard shot me. Austin, go get that prick and chew him up. But don't swallow. You'll get a belly ache."

Austin didn't move. The doctor simply stared at them before he made a small laugh. "She's out of her mind with pain." He gave a short nod before going on. "Yes, she's in so much pain. That's why...I mean, why else would she want you to chew someone up and not swallow?"

He looked so desperate for Austin to agree that he nodded. Austin thought the man had encountered another paranormal in his life and had tried to explain it away just this way. The medic came in and took her away before either man could say any more about what CJ had said. That had been over four hours ago. As soon as she'd gotten to the hospital, they had taken her up to surgery.

"Are you asking me if I killed Solomon?" Austin asked Oliver. "Because I assure you, I didn't. The last I saw of him, he'd just shot my wife."

Agent Oliver sat up then. His eyes were bloodshot and his face was pale. "No, sir. We're not. We just wondered if you might know...one of our other agents is...." The man looked around before continuing in a much lower voice. "We have an agent who is a wolf. I wouldn't have believed it myself, but I saw him morph. He told me you were one too. He said you were a leader."

Austin looked around the small area and didn't feel another wolf. He looked back at the agent. He looked better, Austin thought, but not yet great.

"Alpha. I'm an alpha, and there is no other wolf in this room, other than myself and my family, among your supernaturals. What's his name?" Austin did laugh when the agent looked sharply around the room. He must not have known that there were others around him all the time.

"Other supernaturals," Oliver's voice practically squeaked. "What do you...? What are they and who? I should have been told that I'm working with others."

Austin wouldn't give up the others, but he would let the man know what he was working with. It might come in handy if they needed to speak with the others they dealt with.

"In this room alone you have a vampire, a weretiger, a werepanther, and two shifters." Austin never broke eye contact with the man. "The shifters, before you ask, can shift into nearly any animal there is. And no, I won't tell you who they are. They'll either tell you or not depending on if they ever trust you enough to do so."

Oliver looked around the room again before looking back at Austin. "I suppose you know that I'm not anything. How? How did you know what was in the room with us?"

"Scent. I can smell better than most animals, as can the others. Some have a better sense of smell, some hearing. There are a few who are very good at both. I doubt there's any one of them in this room who doesn't know every word we've said. And we're not a 'what' but a 'who,' Agent Oliver."

He had the good grace to flush. "I'm sorry. This is all so...I know you find it hard to believe, but I do have an open mind. I'm just, it's hard to imagine anyone like you and the others are around. Please forgive me."

Austin nodded. He stood up when his mother came toward him, as did the agent. She looked down the hall and Austin saw the doctor coming toward them. For as much as Austin wanted to run the man down and demand answers, he knew that it would get him thrown out of the hospital, and when his mother was finished kicking his ass, CJ would too. So he waited for the news as he held his breath.

~~~

CJ jerked awake. The pain of the quick movement made her moan, and before she could put her hand over the pain in her belly, Austin was suddenly there. He held her gently but firmly, but it was still very painful.

"You're all right. Shhhh, it's okay, I've got you, babe." She wanted to curl into his warmth, but knew she would hurt more if she did. She gave him a little push and he moved back, but didn't let her go.

"Don't think...." She had to swallow twice, her throat was so sore. "Don't think that's going to get you out of trouble with me. I'm still pissed at you."

His grin made her heart flip, but she felt too weak to get into anything much more than a verbal match with him right now. She looked down at the IV in her hand and saw her ring was missing.

When he'd slipped it on her finger at the wedding, she couldn't believe how beautiful it was. A moonstone surrounded by eight diamonds, each a different hue of blues, gold, and white. The band was engraved with a pair of wolves that were paired nose to nose, their paws touching over a heart. He'd shown her inside the band where each person who had used it had carved the year they'd gotten married. The firstborn had used the wedding band for several generations starting in the early seventeen hundreds. Austin told her they would have it engraved when they got home.

"I have it," he told her when she asked. "They don't want you to wear anything just yet." He sat on the edge of the bed and took her hand. "I've missed you so much."

She looked at the door when it opened. Austin didn't so much as stand in front of her as he'd completely blocked whoever had come in from seeing her. The low growl made the hair on her neck and arms raise.

"I just want to talk to her. I promise I'll make it quick." The man sounded nervous, scared, actually. "Please, Mr.

Force, just let me finish my job and I'll leave you both alone."

"Austin, what's going on?" She touched his arm and felt the muscles ripple beneath her fingers. Her whole body contracted with need and he growled again, this time, she was sure, at her.

"Behave," he whispered to her, then continued toward the man. "This man, this agent Ed Aguilar, was the one who was to be watching over you while this was taking place. He didn't do his job and you got hurt. He wants to ask you what you know, and has been waiting like a vulture for two days to do so."

CJ was surprised that she'd been there two days, but decided that now was probably not the time to say anything about it. Instead, she smoothed her hand down Austin's arm and laced her fingers in his.

"Austin, let the man ask his questions. The sooner he gets this done, the sooner we can be alone and talk. You and I have unfinished business to settle."

His hand flexed in hers slightly before he answered. "All right, but I'm not leaving. He can either ask you with me here or not at all." The agent nodded and Austin glanced back at her. "If you mean bringing you here then that's settled. You were hurt, an ambulance was called, and you were operated on. End of discussion. If you mean anything else, then I'm game." The cheeky bastard winked at her, then turned back to the agent. "Finish, and hurry up."

The questions were mostly about the contact she'd had with Solomon, and then a man named Sims. Also, did she know anyone named Baker? For the most part, she couldn't answer about the latter man. She'd never heard of him and until the lobby, had never met any of them. The only conversation she'd had with Solomon was over the phone prior to that.

"Why did you go down to meet him, Mrs. Force? When you knew that he was the one who stole the truck?" Austin started to speak, but she answered the agent before he could.

"The hotel called to say our wedding pictures were finished. And if you are accusing me of something then you'd better tell me what it is or this conversation is over."

The man shifted on his feet a little, looking very uncomfortable all of a sudden. "No. Nothing like that. We just wondered...that was very strange, don't you think? That you'd meet him after all you—"

"Listen to me, you ignorant prick. I did not meet with Solomon. My wedding pictures were.... You know what? Fuck you. Get out. You said you'd keep me safe, you did not. You said that I'd be okay, that you needed my help. Well, now that Solomon got away, you need someone else to pin this on, and I got news for you, you slimy bastard, it's not going to be me. Now, unless the next words out of your mouth are, 'I'm sorry Mr. and Mrs. Force, for messing up your wedding,' then you, sir, can go to hell."

He stiffened and straightened his tie and jacket before answering her. "You cannot just threaten the federal government, young lady. That is—"

"Austin? Would you please be a dear and throw this pompous ass out? I don't think I can take any more of him."

Austin stood and stretched his neck, then lifted his arms over his head in a full body, almost lazy flex of muscles before he smiled, and not a friendly one either. He took one step as he answered her.

"Yes, love, it would be my—"

Aguilar was out the door before Austin could finish. When the door clicked shut, she looked at Austin and tried to be upset with him, but he looked so disappointed that she burst out laughing.

CHAPTER TWENTY TWO

Phil watched CJ sleep. He'd been in the room twice now and both times she'd had company. He'd asked Austin if he could have a word with her alone and the wolf had told him yes. Phil grinned when he thought about how disgruntled Austin had sounded.

He needed to tell her what he'd done to Solomon. Well, not actually tell her precisely what he'd done, but the general idea. He'd already told Austin—the man deserved to know—but with CJ, he thought he'd play it down a bit. When she cleared her throat, he looked up at her again.

"You look like you might be contemplating the weight of the world and how to get rid of it. Are you all right?"

He took her hand before answering. "Yes. Just waiting for you to wake up. You snore, did you know that?"

"I most certainly do not." He helped her shift in the bed so that she was facing him. "What is it, Phil? Something is bothering you."

"I wanted to make sure you knew that I loved you. Dearly. Though I'd rather you didn't tell your husband that. He's a mite possessive." He grinned when she snorted. "Also, I have to tell you what happened."

"You killed Solomon."

He looked at her, surprised. He knew she was a smart girl, but this really threw him off a bit.

"Yes. Yes, I did. How did you…? Austin told you." He looked to the door and wondered if he could find the man and kick his ass before the man woke up.

"No, he didn't. You were the only one who could have, because Austin never left my side. He would have done it, but you did." He was nodding before she finished. "You did it because he shot me, didn't you?"

"Yes. No one hurts my friends. I went a little…I didn't do it very clean either. I shouldn't have let my temper rule my—"

"I don't care how you did it."

Phil looked at her again. He must have looked as shocked as he felt, because she burst out laughing. He frowned at her.

"The man hurt you and you can laugh. Not very nice, young lady. Now tell me you forgive me and I'll go and let you rest. I guess you're going home tomorrow."

"No." He started to ask her why not when she continued. "No, I mean I want to know how you did it. I want to know that he got what he deserved. You can't sugar coat it either. Tell me."

He started to tell her she was better off not knowing, that he'd gone mad with anger, that he'd acted like the animal he'd always known he could be, but he could see the look in her eye and found he needed to tell her.

"He'd shot you before I could react enough to pull you out of the way. I should have…." He stopped when she growled at him. "Okay. You do know that you sound like Austin when you do that, don't you?"

"Stop stalling and tell me. I'm tired of people treating me like I'm some sort of fragile child that needs to be pampered. When I want to be pampered, I'll fucking ask for it."

Phil laughed and kissed her hand before he nodded. "All right, but it's not pretty. Solomon had just shot you when I snatched him up. I'm not sure which one of us was more startled, him or me. But before I knew it, he and I were in a field several miles from the nearest human."

"You can move really fast because you're a vampire, right? And I guess you're strong too. I guess I should have known that…I'm sorry. Go on."

"He started begging me not to hurt him. I knew he was a wolf, I could smell him. I watched him shift to a partial wolf before I tore into him. Literally tore into him. I felt the beast in me rise up when I thought of you bleeding, and I ripped him apart. He was…I did it fast, tearing his body apart until there was nothing left of him. Then when I had his heart in my hand, I drank from him."

He'd not meant to tell her that part, but he'd been seeing himself tear the man apart and forgot he'd meant to tell her only that Solomon was dead. When she didn't say anything, he looked up at her and could see the tears in her eyes. He didn't want her to be upset with him, but before he could tell her so, she spoke softly.

"I'm sorry you had to do that, Phil. I thank you for it, but I'm sorry. No one should have to live with that, and I want you to know that I love you very much for what you did for us, for Austin and me."

Phil simply stared at her. Never in all his lives had he ever met a woman like her, and doubted that he ever would again. He kissed her hand again and then did something he'd not done for centuries.

"I am an old and powerful vampire, CJ. One of the few that has the power to change a human from mortal to immortal without changing you to vampire. I will offer you this boon as my friend for both you and Austin so that you may have many, many years together and beget many children together. I offer this to you because I would spend eternity with you both as my friends."

She smiled at him. "I'll ask Austin. I'm sure he'll have an opinion about it. But for now…are you all right? Will you…can you live with what you did for me?"

"Yes, love. Yes, I can." He hugged her to him and then stood up. "I hope someday that I meet a woman like you. Maybe a little less bossy and opinionated, but other than that, just like you."

He left her then as he could hear someone coming down the hall and with a quick sniff of the air, knew it was Austin.

He was going home. Phil needed to get away from the Forces for a few days, especially Holly.

~~~

CJ watched Austin walk into the room like a man on a mission. She glanced down at the watch they'd given her yesterday along with her ring, and she was surprised that it was nearly two in the morning. She smiled when he came into the room and kissed her.

"You're awake. Ah, Phil's been here. I can smell him on your skin." His tongue lapped at the area where Phil had kissed her cheek. "I wish he'd not mark you like he does. I know he can't help it, but you can't drive me crazy like that."

Her skin seemed to come alive when he touched her. She moaned softly when he licked the area behind her ear then nipped at her lobe. His own moan felt warm against her skin, and she reached up to pull him to her mouth. When they pulled away, neither of them was breathing very well.

"You keep that up and I'm going to go against all my own rules and take you right here. I'd like nothing better than to fill you with my cock hard and fast. And when you smell like you do...." He buried his nose in her shoulder. "All hot and wet, I can't help but want to taste you as well."

Her body shivered and she felt it expand. "Austin, I want you now. Do you think we could make love without being caught?"

He growled, something he seemed to do a lot, and reached up and unsnapped the gown from her shoulder. "We shouldn't, but I need to taste you. I need to come inside of you and hear you scream out my name. But we can't. You don't know how to come quietly, so you'll have to suffer. Unless...." When he didn't finish, she wanted to scream at him.

"Unless what? Austin, don't tease me like this. I need to feel you inside of me like a woman needs chocolate. Tell me."

"I don't want to hurt your belly, but I can make you come. Would you like that? Would you like to come, baby?" He was moving his mouth along her collarbone and toward her breast. She wanted to beg him to do whatever it took, but before she could answer, he took her nipple into his mouth.

His hand came over her mouth just as she took a deep breath. He didn't press hard, but he did make her remember to be quiet. When he suckled hard at her nipple, she nearly came up off the bed.

"Austin, please. I need you. I need more of you."

He shifted on the bed and settled between her legs by sitting on his knees. "Lift your gown up. I'm going to be gentle with you, but you have to come fast. I'm not sure I'll last long if I don't taste you."

His voice sent shivers over her body and she felt her pussy gush. She lifted the gown slowly and was glad that after her shower earlier she'd put on her prettiest panties. His breath catching had her wanting to tease him a bit more.

Holding up the gown with one hand, she ran her free hand along the top of her mound covered by the bright red lace. She nearly came when he spread her legs wider and moved to within a few inches of her pussy.

"Touch yourself for me. I want to watch you masturbate for me."

She slid her fingers into her panties and along the slit of her nether lips. She didn't touch herself yet, neither could he see what she was doing, but his breath on her thighs made her bolder. When she felt his hands on her hips, she knew he was going to rip the lace from her and nearly cried out when he did it.

His fingers opened her further and she could feel her juices run down her ass. CJ knew she was soaking the bed beneath her and didn't care.

"Slide your fingers into your pussy for me. Then feed me. I want you to feed me your cream." She did as he asked, and when his fingers suckled at her fingers covered in her wetness, she watched him. "Hmm, you taste like heaven. Again, CJ. Give me more."

She slid her fingers deep this time, and touched her clit. The small brush of her thumb sent her body into spasms of pleasure and had her moaning. When she moved her other hand down to do it again, Austin stilled her hand with his and took her thumb into his mouth.

"Not yet. I want to be able to see your pussy when you come, and if you come too quickly then I'll not be ready." He moved closer to her and she could feel his breath on her clit. "Come for me, baby. Fuck yourself and come."

She moved her thumb to her clit, gathered a bit of her cream, and used it to rub on herself. Soon she was dancing on the bed to the time of her thumb. Over and over she rubbed the hard nubbin until she could feel her climax beginning to build, but she couldn't bring herself over the edge.

"Austin, I'm so close. Help me. Please." He moved his fingers from her slit that he'd held open and down her ass. She nearly protested that she wanted him inside of her, not her ass, when he entered her dark hole.

The pain-pleasure sent her over the edge fast. Her entire body came from her head to her toes. There was a slight pain in her belly, but nothing compared to the climax that rippled through her. And when Austin's mouth covered her, she came again, her legs tightening around his head until she felt him pull them apart.

"Again," he commanded, and she did, coming apart and then mashing together again as a bundle of sensations made her whimper and moan. He moved up her body as she was still jerking from the incredible climax. As he unsnapped his pants and freed his cock, she leaned up, but was stayed by his hand on her shoulder.

"I want to come on you. Lower your gown and let me come on your breasts." She did as he asked and watched, mesmerized, as he fisted his cock and a stream of pearly cum dripped from the tip. "Christ, I'm not going to last. Baby, touch yourself for me. Lift those pretty tits up for me and watch me."

Cupping her breasts for him, she moaned when the first hot splash hit her. Rubbing her nipples with his cum, she nearly came again. When she reached out and gathered some on her fingers and took it to her mouth, she heard Austin growl at her to open her mouth.

The next stream of cum filled her mouth. Before she could swallow, he was coming again and again. His hot seed covered her face and breasts. When his fingers tangled in her hair, she took his cock into her mouth and he fucked her hard. Moaning around his cock, she took him deep, swallowing around him and tasting. Sliding her hands down to her pussy, she pinched her clit and felt the tremors of another climax take her even as he pulled from her mouth.

Austin leaned his head against the headboard above her, panting hard. CJ wasn't sure how he'd managed it, but his thighs were on either side of her and his cock only a few inches from her mouth. She shifted her head and licked the last of his cum from the tip. She was rewarded by his cock jerking and Austin moaning at her.

"Don't. I swear to Christ you're going to kill me." He moved down and off the bed. Leaving his pants undone, he went to her bathroom and she could hear water running. When he returned, he had done up his pants and had a washcloth with him.

He kissed her quickly then began to clean her up. She was too relaxed to protest and wasn't really sure she would have anyway. He helped her change her gown, and giggled when he stuffed the one she'd had on in the case she was taking home.

"I only meant to give you pleasure, and you nearly took my head off. What am I going to do with you when I get you home?"

"Hopefully more of that." She laughed when he glared at her. "Oh come on, you know you enjoyed that. I loved it."

He didn't answer her, but did climb into the bed with her. "Behave, or I'll spank your bottom."

She was nearly asleep when she thought of something that had been bothering her. "Austin, why didn't you change me when I was hurt?"

He was quiet for so long she didn't think he'd answer. "I wanted it to be because we both wanted it to happen, not because it was a way to save your life. The doctor said you weren't in grave danger, but you had lost a great deal of blood. I couldn't…didn't…want to do it then. Not without you knowing what was going to happen."

She looked over at him. "Happen? You said you'd have to hurt me, bite me. What else is going to happen? Tell me please."

"You're going to hurt. Not just hurt, but scream in pain from when…I'll have to bite you deep, CJ, deeper than I've ever bitten anyone except in battles. I don't know if I can do it to you. I don't….Then there's Dallas's part. He'll have to bite you as well. He's my…our enforcer, and you'd have to accept him as well."

She rolled to her side and thought for a moment. "Dallas will be a part of me as well then? He'll be a part of my wolf too?"

"Yes. He'll bite you, but only to give you his essences. I'll change you. He'll bite you because your wolf, when she comes, will need to be able to dominate his. Your wolf will know his. Understand?"

Did she? She wasn't sure. It was going to be hard enough having one wolf bite her, but two, she wasn't so sure. She loved Austin, but this was big.

"Could I die?"

He shifted on the bed and brought her around to face him. "I won't have you dying on me. You'll not think those things, do you understand me? I need you in my life. I love you and you'll live, or so help me, CJ, I will kick your ass."

CHAPTER TWENTY THREE

Austin watched his people as they gathered around the open field. He was terrified he was going to screw this up, and nearly called them all to order and told them that he'd...he'd what? Changed his mind? No, he hadn't done that, but he didn't want to hurt his wife. He didn't think he'd be able to do this, to cause her pain. He was just standing to call it off when Dallas clapped him on the shoulder.

"Don't do it. If you do, CJ will murder you in your sleep. And I'll help her." Austin looked at his brother. "I mean it. It's been four months since you introduced her to them all, and they want her as their alpha. Hell, CJ was pissed enough last moon when you didn't do it."

"She'll hurt, and I can't do that do her. She's my life. She's—"

"She's going to knock you on your hard head if you don't buck up and do this. Austin Force, do you love this woman or not?" His mom stood on his other side and he turned to look at her as she asked.

"Yes, with all my heart. But she may die."

Dallas hugged his brother tight. "She may, but you will if you don't do this. I just left her and she said to tell you if you changed your mind again, she was going to have Phil change her to a vamp. She won't have you being stupid, she said. Now, do I go and find the blood sucker, or are you going to make her your woman?"

Austin looked back at the house and then at his brother. He knew he was right. CJ had told him last week and then again this morning that if he didn't change her, she'd go to Phil. She'd do it too, just to piss him off. He nodded once, and then Dallas hugged him again and went to get CJ.

Austin went to the center of the field and heard everyone start to quiet. He took a deep breath and faced the more than three hundred wolves he'd come to know and love.

"Tonight, I take a mate." The crowd's cheers were deafening. When they calmed a little, he continued. "I take my mate tonight, this night of the first of the new spring and new beginnings. I welcome you all to watch as I commit her to one of us and take her as my full mate. Hopefully soon we will have cubs to join the already growing pack."

Austin felt her enter the circle and turned to look at her. His breath caught when he saw what she was wearing. He fell in love with her all over again.

She wore the ceremonial robe of his kind. His family had been wearing one like this for generations, and his mother had worn the one that CJ now had on. The color of their pack, the dark silk hugged her body like a skin and he felt his cock harden at the thought of what she may or, in this case, may not have on beneath it. She walked toward him and smiled.

"You ready for this, big boy?" She kissed his mouth quickly then stepped back before asking him again.

"Yes. No. I don't know. I love you, CJ. You are all that I am and more." He pulled her to him, much to the happiness of those around them. "You can't die on me, love. I won't...I'll die without you."

"I'm not going to die. I'm going to be your love. Your alpha person. Now, how about we get this show on the road?" She untied the robe and let it fall to the ground. She took a deep breath, turned to the crowd, and smiled.

He wrapped his arms around her, hugged her to him, and kissed the warm place between her shoulder and neck. He watched as his brother began to disrobe too.

When Dallas was naked, he shifted. Austin had seen him and another do this a million times over his lifetime, and was seeing it for the first time through CJ's eyes. When she leaned back against him, he felt her tremble. Dallas moved toward them slowly.

"He'll bite you in the leg first. Not enough to cause you great harm, but it will hurt. He will need to draw blood." She nodded against his chin where she was tucked.

Dallas leaned against her leg and she reached down and scratched him behind the ears. "Do it, Dallas. Please, don't try to work up to it, just bite."

Austin felt her stiffen, but she didn't make a sound when Dallas bit. His teeth made a deep mark on her thigh that hopefully, before the moon lowered in the night sky, would heal and not leave a scar.

"His next bite will be to your arm. This one will be deeper and much longer. You don't want to jerk from his mouth or he'll hurt you. I'm so sorry about this, love."

"Hush," she told him, and put out her arm for Dallas. With a quick nod, he struck. His fangs bit deep into her flesh and again, she didn't make a sound. Austin pulled her closer to his body when she wobbled a bit unsteadily. Dallas whimpered.

"The next bite will be to your belly." When he started to tell her how sorry he was again, she stomped down on his foot with her bare one. He stopped and continued to tell her what was going to happen next. "The bite will be deep. When he pulls away, I will lie you down on the ground and shift. Dallas will shift back to human and hold you for me.

My bites will follow the same pattern but will be deeper and I will linger more."

She held up her hand when Dallas moved forward. Austin held his breath. If she stopped this now, she may die. He wanted to tell her so, but she pulled away slightly and put her hand on Dallas's head.

"I am your alpha, your brother's mate. But I take you into my heart and into my soul for all my lifetimes. As your sister, I will love you more for what you have done for us both tonight, Dallas." She leaned down and kissed his nose, then rose and leaned against Austin once more. With a quick kiss to his mouth, she nodded. "I'm ready."

Dallas didn't hesitate, but lunged forward and sank his fangs deep into her soft flesh. The only sound she made was a small cry of pain, then she closed her eyes. After what seemed an eternity to him but was only a few minutes, Dallas let her go and backed away. His shift was quick and he was suddenly standing beside her.

Dallas helped him lower her gently to the ground. Austin could smell her blood, hot and fresh. Her heart was pounding in her chest and he could hear her blood rushing through her veins. When she smiled at them both, Austin felt his heart soar.

He quickly stripped off his own robe and shifted. He knew he had to do it; he had to bite hard and continue to do so until she was wolf. He hesitated for a few seconds, and when she looked up at him and smiled, he saw her love for him shining through.

"Austin, if you let me lie here naked in front of all these people for two more seconds, I'm going to cut that impressive dick of yours off and feed it to the cat. Now, change me, or so help me, you'll be very sore for a very, very long time."

He licked her wound and then, steeling himself for her screams, he bit. The bone in her leg splintered under his teeth. Her leg trembled beneath his mouth, but with a small soothing noise from Dallas, she quieted. Austin fell in love with her all over. As soon as he moved to her arm, he could feel the change starting. She was his and would soon truly be his mate.

Her arm raised for him, Dallas held her hand while Austin licked again. This time when he bit her, he heard her cry out, but she quieted once again. Austin covered her with his body, trying to keep her warm as her blood poured into his mouth. When Austin shifted to her side to take her belly, he looked up at Dallas.

"She's out. Her heart is slow, but not dangerously so. When you bite her again, she may cry out more, but you can't stop now. Hurry, Austin...claim your mate."

The bite he was going to give her belly would be deep. It would puncture her intestines and her kidney. He knew that if he did this right, all the wounds would heal, but he was terrified of them not healing. He felt her pain in his heart as if it were his own.

Leaning forward, he snapped his teeth into her and felt her stiffen then cry out. He watched the tears fall down her cheeks. When her eyes opened, he saw the pain there, but he also saw her love. When her hand fell across his head then slid down to his neck, he felt her fingers tangle there.

"I love you, Austin Force." Then her eyes closed.

~~~

CJ woke to the sound of cheering. She was covered in a blanket, and knew she was naked beneath it with the cold ground under her. She started to sit up, but was pushed back down and looked to see Nancy sitting next to her.

"Gather your strength slowly. If you rise now, those idiots will expect you to fall over. I want them to see you at your best, as I'm sure you do as well."

Oddly, she felt no pain, but she did lay still. Her body felt...she thought strange was the wrong word, but she couldn't think of anything better. She listened to try and find Austin, and was surprised to realize she knew exactly where he was.

"Is Austin standing near a tree with Dallas and…Gordon? I can feel him there and, well, I was going to say see him, but that's not right, is it?"

Nancy laughed. "Yes to both. He's near his brothers, and it is right that you can see him. You'll be able to speak to him as well. Visualize him in your mind and speak to him." She laughed again. "I wish I could see his face when you reach for him. I think he thinks you're still resting."

CJ reached out and felt the snap of the connection like a rubber band being stretched then let go. *"Hello, love. How are you doing?"*

She felt his surprise. Not only that, but his relief. *"I'm fine now that you've decided to come around. I love you, CJ Force."*

"Your mother seems to think I should rest a bit longer, but all I can think about is your naked body over me and then your cock…. Christ, no one else can hear us, can they?"

His laughter was warm and soothing. She felt him coming toward her, his need pressing into her from their connection.

"No, no one can hear us. Though you'll be able to talk to Dallas this way, I'll be privy to that, as you will be with my conversations with him. As soon as you shift, you'll be able to communicate with the other wolves on another path all together." He was very close now. *"CJ, are you ready for the final part of your change?"*

"Yes. Should I sit up now, or wait until my manly man comes to pick me up?" She took his hand when he held it out to her and he pulled her from the ground. He took her mouth in an almost savage kiss that had her giving as good as she got. When he pulled back, she could feel his cock pressing hard into her belly.

"I want you. I want you more than I've ever wanted anything in my life," he whispered in her ear just before he nipped at her neck.

Her body reacted to his. She felt her nipples tighten and her pussy clench with need. Even as he pulled her close again, she could feel her juices trickle down her thighs. His growl only made her wetter, and she had to hold him before she fell back to the earth and took him deep inside of her. Forgetting that he could read her thoughts for a moment, she nearly came from the feelings she was getting from him, and he growled again.

"Stop that. If you keep that up, we'll never get to go on our run, and the moon is at its peak." He kissed her again then pulled back from her. He turned toward the crowd still gathered there. "My mate. Your alpha. Tonight we shift and together, we run." He turned back to her and looked at her. "You can do this. Think of the wolf like I told you. See her in your mind and call for her. She'll know what to do. Call to her and she'll change you."

CJ closed her eyes and tried to think of a wolf. She wanted her to come so badly because Austin wanted her to shift. But it seemed the harder she tried, the more elusive she became. Then suddenly, there she was.

It was startling at first to see her standing in front of her…not really a part of her, yet she was. When she snarled at CJ, all she could do was smile. Then she felt her body begin to change.

There was pain…incredible at first, but as the seconds seemed to stretch out, the pain shifted into something soft, something she could handle. The wolf, her wolf, snarled again and seemed to leap at her. CJ welcomed her with open arms, and suddenly, she was there.

She opened her eyes to a view that frightened her. Sounds from around her made her wince and growl. She took a step back and was startled to find that the earth felt softer, her feet felt…she looked down at her hands and was surprised to find paws.

"Austin," she cried out. She tried to back away, but something held her.

"Shhhh, I have you. You're fine…more than fine. Love, you did it. Christ, you're more beautiful than I ever dreamed you'd be. And white. We've not seen a white wolf in…well hell, baby, I don't know when. You're all right, honey. I'm right here. I'm going to shift now, and you'll be able to communicate with me. Just be careful not to get too far away tonight. I want to keep you close."

She'd done it? She was a wolf? She wanted to see her…herself, she supposed. But before she could figure out a way to find a mirror, she felt the moment that Austin shifted.

Her wolf seemed to come alive, and before she knew it, they were running along the forest floor like children. She noticed the others around her, around them, but didn't pay them any mind. She felt free, wild, and incredibly strong. When Austin started to herd her and box her in, she wanted to bite him and make him let her go, but then she noticed they were alone deep in the forest, and she was suddenly afraid.

"Come to me. I need you now. Come and submit to me and let me fuck you."

His voice was harsh, and though the demand should have made her want to rebel, she found herself wanting him to dominate her, to take her. Before she knew it, he was on her, his body covering hers.

His cock was there, just at her entrance, when she felt his teeth sink into her neck. She yipped in pain, but held still. When his cock entered her, she came hard and fast, her body ready for him immediately. His low growl of warning had her lifting into his thrust even as she knew she should be submissive.

Austin took her hard, pounding into her deeper than she'd ever felt him. When he lifted his head and howled, she could feel his cum fill her, his body quivering inside as he filled her. He didn't let her up, but kept his weight on her for several more seconds before he spoke again.

"You're in heat. Christ, I want to fuck you again like this, but I want my cock deep in your pussy too. Shift for me, CJ. Shift so that I can fill you with my seed."

It took her a few minutes to shift. Her wolf, now that she was out, didn't seem to want to come back in. She didn't blame her. It had been fun and freeing. When she finally became human, Austin, as a human, fell on her like he was a starving man and she his first meal.

His cock strained from his groin. She licked her lips and started to reach for him, wanting desperately to take him into her mouth. But he flipped her to her belly and pulled her hips up to meet his. In a powerful surge forward, he entered her.

His cock touched her in ways she'd never felt before. Every time he pulled free of her, she rocked back to take him in, and when he plowed forward, he nearly took her to the ground. His cock was thickening in her. She felt him stretch her walls and her sheath felt each stroke of his cock. When he stilled behind her, she felt his fingers tighten at her hips as he held her still.

"I'm going to fill you. I'm going to plant my seed inside of you and create a child. Now, right now, tell me you want this. Tell me that you'll accept my seed, or so help me if I move again, you'll have no choice."

His child, hers. She wanted his baby growing inside her more than anything in this world. Her answer was to push back and tighten around him. With a harsh growl, he leaned over her, his arms on either side of her arms. He began fucking her hard, taking her to a place she'd never been. When she was close, close enough to almost touch it, to feel it, he bit her shoulder and she came apart, his cum bringing her to peak again and again.

CHAPTER TWENTY FOUR

CJ woke in bed. She was alone, but she could feel warmth on the pillow next to her head and pulled it to her nose to inhale his scent. When she rolled to her back, she thought about last night and what he'd done...what they'd done. Running her hand over her belly, she thought about his child growing there. She looked up when she felt Austin near.

"You will know soon if you're pregnant. I hope so. I want to see you large with my cub." He moved toward her as he spoke. "I have something for you. My mother took it last night and I thought you'd enjoy it."

He handed her a sheet of paper. When it touched her fingers, she realized it was photo paper and had a moment of panic when she wondered if Nancy had seen them in the forest having sex. Her face heated up at that thought.

"After all we've done to each other, you still blush. I love to watch your skin heat up. You've no idea what that does to me." He cupped the back of her head and pulled her to his mouth for a quick but very sensual kiss. "Look at the picture before I throw you back on the bed and take you again."

It was a wolf, a white wolf standing in a field. CJ thought she'd never seen anything more beautiful than this creature. When she looked up at Austin, he was looking at her, not the picture.

"It's you. Your wolf." He pointed to the darker wolf behind the white one. "That's me. The larger black wolf is me. Mom said that we looked like dark and light together, and to see us run was beauty in itself."

"I'm white? But I don't understand. I thought because you changed me and you're black…." CJ looked up at him. "I don't understand."

"I asked the elder. She said that it didn't matter what I wanted you to be, that Mother Earth decided you'd be white. It's a very rare thing for a wolf, a turned wolf, to be white. Sometimes there are ones born of a full-blooded pair, but she said that it has never happened in all her life for a white wolf to be made. She said you're a gift to our pack. My gift as well."

CJ looked at the picture again. She ran her finger down the wolf's coat. "Won't this be hard for me to hunt with you? I mean, I don't know a great deal about hunting, but won't I sort of stick out like a sore thumb?"

Austin's laugh made her look at him. "Ah, love, we no longer hunt to survive, but eat when we want. Your coat of white will make you stand out, but then as my alpha person, you'll stand and shine anyway."

She smiled at the use of her name. She'd put her foot down at being called a bitch. She didn't care if it was what she was. Alpha person was the one thing that he'd given her, but she'd have to put up with being called "bitch" by the pack. She agreed so long as when they were alone, he'd refrain from calling her that.

"So, I'm a white pregnant wolf about to have a litter of cubs. Sure, why not. I suppose you want me to knit booties too?"

He smiled, but didn't say anything. She found herself back on the bed before she could ask him again. When his mouth covered her nipple and bit, she nearly came up off the bed and moaned at the same time. A pounding at the door made her groan.

Austin snarled, then commanded whoever was there to go away.

"I can't, alpha. Your mother said...she said to get your...sir, I'm only repeating what she said. She said for you to get your pants on and get down here to tell her goodbye. She is moving to the little house now."

CJ nearly fell over him getting up. She had a plan of her own and it didn't involve her new mother-in-law moving out. She snatched up her robe and was out the door right behind her husband. She was in front of the door when Nancy moved toward it.

"Oh no, you don't. You're not going anywhere...at least not to the little house." CJ held up her hand when everyone started to talk at once. "The house in the meadow is completed. I had extra crews put in just so it would be done now. There are enough rooms in the house for several families, and since ours is expanding by leaps and bounds, I need you to stay with me."

Nancy seemed ready to speak, but shook her head slightly before she did. "I wanted you to have...you need your privacy, child. And the house, running the pack is now your responsibility. I need to do this for you."

CJ moved forward, put her arms around Nancy, and put her mouth to her ear. "I'm going to have a baby. I need you. Please don't leave me now. I need you to come and stay with us, for me."

Nancy pulled back and looked at her, then at her belly. She then looked at her son with wide eyes. "You...she...when?"

Austin laughed and gathered both of them in his arms. "Yes, her, last night. Will you please come and stay with us? She'll need you now more than ever. I have plans for the little house anyway. I'm going to use it for a guesthouse. A house for packs to come and visit. We talked it...CJ and I talked it over last week. We want you to come to the house and stay with us and help us."

Nancy stared at both them for so long that CJ was sure she was going to say no. But when her head nodded, Austin picked her up and swung her around the room. The rest of the family, her family now, CJ thought, came running into the room.

~~~

Phil watched the move. He'd helped as much as he could, but he was trying to get the paperwork ready for Austin and CJ so that everything was now theirs and no longer each person's. Plus, he didn't think he could be so close to Holly without kissing her.

He watched her flirt with another male, and it was all he could do not to go and drain the man. Phil knew that he had no rights, none at all when it came to the headstrong wolf, but he wanted them...wanted them in the worst sort of way. Just as he was thinking of going to her, he nearly leapt out of his skin when Connor, Austin's younger brother, came up behind him and slapped him on the back.

"I thought you bloodsuckers were supposed to be this almighty predator or something. What has you so distracted?" Phil tried to turn away, but the man was much smarter than he'd thought. "Ah, her. She's my sister, you know."

Phil tried to turn away again. "I have no idea what you're talking about. I was just going to go home and finish up—"

"You don't want her?" Phil turned back to Connor. "My sister, I'm guessing she's your mate. So what is it, you don't want her?"

Phil looked back at Holly, then at her brother. "I'm a vampire."

"Yeah, I got that. But what I don't know is why you keep running from her. She's a bit rough around the edges, but I'm guessing you know that. So the only thing I can think is that you don't want her."

Phil cocked his head at Connor. "You mean you don't care that.... She's my mate and we're mixed blood. I'll drink from her when—"

"Yeah, too much information. I know what you do. But you still haven't answered my question. We can all see that she's your mate. Hell, Phil, we'd have to be blind not to see the way you look at her and she looks at you."

"She looks at me?" Phil turned back to look at Holly. He didn't know she looked at him. That opened— "What does Austin say about this? Or your mother? I'm assuming you all know."

Connor threw back his head and laughed. "Yeah, we all know. I wouldn't be much of a cop if I didn't notice things. As for Austin, I don't think he'll have an issue with it, or my mom. The one you have to worry about is her. Holly can be a bit...well, you know what I mean. You're going to need a lot of stamina for that one."

Phil knew that. He'd watched her tear into a guy just yesterday who'd tried to get her into a corner. Phil had stood to go to her rescue when the man was suddenly across the room. She'd flipped him over and threw him so quickly all Phil could do was stare. She'd looked right at him when she noticed he was looking. Her look said to just try it and see what he got.

He decided he wanted to see what he'd get. Mustering up courage to face the woman he'd loved for nearly a decade, he walked across the room and jerked her around to face him. Before she could say a word, he pulled her body to his and kissed her.

Her mouth was warm and wet, and when his tongue begged for entrance, she let him in on a sigh. Phil pulled her body flush with his and nearly groaned when she pressed against him. It was all he could do not to throw her to the ground and take her. When she started to pull away, he shifted again and pressed her against the wall he'd moved them toward with his speed.

"Don't, you can't…this has to stop," she said when he moved down her neck. "Phil, you have to…Christ."

His teeth grazed her pounding pulse. He wanted to taste her, sink his teeth into her hot blood and taste, but he licked the beating pulse and moved back up to her mouth again. When she pushed him back, he let her but didn't let her go.

"Holly, I need you. Now. I need to take you now." Her groan made him rock into her softness. "Holly, your family said it's okay. I want to—"

He almost realized his mistake too late. When she dug her nails—claws, he supposed—into his shoulders, he winced at the pain, but still didn't let her go.

"They said its okay for you to fuck me? Well how nice for you. Did they tell you that it's okay to take me against the wall, or didn't they tell you how to do it?"

He tried to correct what he'd meant, but that only seemed to piss her off more. "Holly, I'm a vampire. I didn't think…your brothers are very protective of you, and I didn't think they'd let me…."

"Oh no, finish. Wouldn't let you what? Fuck me? Kiss me? What? Tell me what they wouldn't let you do?"

"Claim you as my mate."

ABOUT THE AUTHOR

I woke up one morning and decided to give play time to the people in my head who were keeping me awake. Little did I know that they would be so relentless and want their time right now! I wrote for the pure joy of it and to entertain my family and friends. But mostly it was to get more than an hour of sleep without a story playing out. Of course, the more I write, the more they want. So...well, as a result of sleepless days (I work through the night as a gun toting grandma – nope not a vigilantly but an armed security guard) I have lots of stories written.

Hello! My name is Kathi Barton and I'm an author. I have been married to my very best friend Sonny for at times seems several lifetimes – in a good way, honey. And together we have three wonderful children and then the ones we brought into the world - Paul and Dale Barton, Jason and Wendy Barton and Danielle and Ben Conklin. They have given us seven of the greatest treasures on Earth. They don't live at home seven days a week! No, seriously, seven grandchildren – Gavin, Spring, Ben, Trinity, Sarah, Kelly and Kian.

www.ingramcontent.com/pod-product-compliance
Lightning Source LLC
Chambersburg PA
CBHW030304180626
46810CB00003B/908